Rising. . .with bright n ✔ **KU-483-436**
Stars. . .*that work their own special magic*

The last thing Ben needed was to spend time with Kate socially.

Pretending to himself that he wasn't really looking at her. Denying that he'd felt a stab of something utterly wonderful when they'd met on the moor.

When he'd seen her with John Smith last night he had felt resentment deep inside. He'd wanted to get rid of the wretched man so that he could have her all to himself—even though he knew this was the last thing he should wish for.

He felt such surges of anger, and all because he'd been tempted to overstep the mark, and he could never do that. . .

One special month, four special authors. Some of the names you might recognise, like Jessica Matthews, whose book this month is also the beginning of a trilogy. Lucy Clark and Jenny Bryant offer their second books, while **Poppy's Passion** *introduces Helen Shelton.*

Rising Stars. . .*catch them while you can!*

Dear Reader

I hope you will enjoy A REMEDY FOR
HEARTACHE. I certainly enjoyed writing it. I am
also very happy at the moment, because Harlequin
Mills & Boon chose this book for publication.

The day I first learnt that I was to become one of
their authors was an exciting one. It opened up a
whole new life for me, where I could go on doing
what I love best—writing novels that come from
the heart!

Now I have so many new characters and stories
jostling in my head that I can hardly wait to bring
them alive on the page. When this happens, I
would like to bring you pleasure by sharing them
with you.

So, goodbye for now. I wish you many hours of
happy reading.

Jenny Bryant

Recent titles by the same author:

A LOVING PARTNERSHIP

A REMEDY
FOR HEARTACHE

BY
JENNY BRYANT

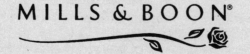

MILLS & BOON®

First published in Great Britain 1997
Harlequin Mills & Boon Limited,
Eton House, 18-24 Paradise Road, Richmond, Surrey TW9 1SR

© Jenny Bryant 1997

ISBN 0 263 80376 7

Set in Times 10 on 12 pt. by
Rowland Phototypesetting Limited
Bury St Edmunds, Suffolk

03-9709-45381-D

Printed and bound in Great Britain
by Mackays of Chatham PLC, Chatham

CHAPTER ONE

'GOOD luck, love! We're really going to miss your sparkling green eyes! So come back and see us some time!'

Kate Frinton couldn't distinguish this voice from all the others, so she just smiled at the crowd standing outside the surgery to wave her off.

'Will do!' she said, knowing that it was unlikely that she ever would return to this sprawling Midlands town. There were too many memories here. Too much pain.

Driving off at last, she joined a motorway and took the route to Devon—trying to forget the agony of the past few months. When she finally came to terms with the anger, still lying deep inside her, she'd be able to live again, wouldn't she? Then the silent question of 'What if?' would be forgotten for ever.

When she eventually left the motorway she headed for more pleasant country roads until she was skirting the edge of Dartmoor. At that moment she experienced the same frisson of excitement she'd known as a child on holiday in the West Country.

Now, seeing the early signs of spring, she at last dismissed her doubts about joining the twin practices which were at opposite ends of Lanbury, a village which all the brochures described as picturesque.

New Barling was the more recent, designed to serve a council estate which was still being built. The Rowans was at the far edge of Lanbury—a Victorian house where

Maurice Gilmore, the senior partner, also lived. Now widowed—and quite near to retirement, he'd said—he was looked after by a housekeeper.

They were both small practices—so different from the one Kate had left behind. Here she would have time to see patients as people, she thought. Not merely as cases. She would also be able to breathe clean air—a far cry from the industrial smog she'd become used to.

In Devon, which had always held a kind of magic for her, she would actually begin to feel whole again. Then that terrible image of David would no longer haunt her dreams.

At last, turning into a track running across the moor towards the village, she caught sight of something in the distance which, she thought, might be an ancient standing stone. Yet it puzzled her. It should really have been part of a Stone Age circle—not left on its own like this.

But as she drew nearer the shape suddenly moved. She smiled to herself ruefully. What she'd seen was no ancient landmark—but a man!

Wearing a grey anorak and holding a large pad against his chest, he seemed to be sketching. Stopping at times, he stooped down to examine something in the grass before he straightened up again.

An artist, perhaps? Or a surveyor? Whatever he was, Kate thought that he was one of the tallest men she'd ever seen. Well over six feet, she reckoned. And broad, too. With wide lean shoulders and a shock of dark blond hair above an intriguing face, he was breathtakingly attractive.

Steady on, girl! she murmured to herself. This was the kind of scenario she just didn't want. Hadn't she learnt the hard way? Sworn to push herself entirely into patient care now that she had escaped from her nightmare? Breaking off a relationship with a man she had once thought perfect had been the hardest thing she'd ever done. No way did she want to go through all that again!

Nevertheless, she couldn't prevent herself from slowing down and then stopping as she reached this giant of a man. And before she knew it she was winding down the window and asking him—quite unnecessarily—if she was on the right road to Lanbury.

He smiled at her, his sensitive and mobile mouth curving into an attractive half-moon shape that suddenly made her heart race. For heaven's sake, stop acting like a fool, she told herself sternly. Then found that she was unable to look away from him.

'Yes, you go straight on,' he said, his voice deep and pleasant.

He stopped speaking suddenly, and then the strangest thing happened. He stared straight at her, and the attractive smile left his face, making him seem bleak. Lost, somehow. And his eyes, which were the deepest blue she thought she had ever seen, became almost navy as they glared at her. As if he'd taken a sudden dislike to her, for heaven's sake!

But a moment later the darkness had gone, leaving only a slight frown.

'Thanks for your help,' she said politely, unable to control a cold edge to her voice.

Resenting his unspoken criticism which she considered entirely uncalled-for, she drove away quickly—determined to put the incident behind her. She would probably never see the man again, anyway. Then he and his very obvious mood swings could be forgotten. For all she cared he could remain a man of mystery!

But a small devil inside began to taunt her. And she realised that she was actually hoping that they might meet again.

At last, telling herself to stop behaving like some stupid teenager instead of a woman of twenty-seven, she drove the car up a steep hill, then coasted down to meet a cobbled street where the village of Lanbury began. Finally she stopped in front of the solid stone house she had inspected after her interview. And she suddenly smiled at the thought of meeting Mrs Marsden again, the plump and comfortable landlady who'd insisted on being called 'Tilly'.

She was just like clotted cream, Kate thought. Full of goodness and absolutely delicious—but a little went a long way. Now a widow, she lived on the ground floor after her son Bert had turned the upper rooms into a furnished flat which she rented out.

The moment they'd met she had offered to 'keep Dr Frinton clean and tidy', for which Kate had thanked her gratefully. But when she'd also offered to cook for her Kate had refused—trying to be tactful and hoping that the woman wouldn't be offended. But Tilly had smiled, saying that she fully understood Kate's need for privacy, and at that moment Kate had known that she would be happy here.

It was also when she'd learnt that for some time the villagers would think of her as a 'Grockle'. At least until they had accepted her as their new GP.

'And when is that likely to happen?' Kate had asked, already making up her mind to overcome local prejudice with her own brand of cheerfulness.

'Shouldn't take long! Not if you give 'em that dazzlin' smile, me dear,' Tilly had chuckled.

So that was that, Kate thought now as she left the car and rang her new landlady's bell. It was up to her to win the locals over. Just as if she were a foreigner in some remote land, she thought with amusement.

Tilly greeted her as if she had known her for ever. Then she ushered her into her own downstairs flat with a flourish, as if her new lodger were some kind of VIP, and invited her to sit at the living-room table while she brought in a pot of tea and something she called 'thunder and lightning'.

'What on earth is that?' Kate asked.

'You'll soon see, me dear,' Tilly said, giving her a mysterious wink before she disappeared.

Kate eventually discovered what thunder and lightning really was when she found herself biting into scones piled high with Devonshire cream and dripping with golden syrup. Not good for the cholesterol level, she thought. But wonderfully smooth on the tongue.

After a conversation which consisted entirely of Tilly asking personal questions, with Kate carefully fielding her answers, she realised that there wasn't much of her private life left hidden. But somehow it didn't seem to matter. Kate, who had lost her parents long ago, found herself confiding in this woman without a qualm because she soon realised that, far from being a gossip, Tilly was a serious listener.

In the end Kate had told her many things that she'd kept to herself for years. Like the competition she'd always felt between herself and her three older brothers—also doctors—who were now high-powered specialists. And how she had at last managed to overcome her sense of inferiority, finally making her own way in the medical world.

But she did manage to avoid speaking about her love life, even though Tilly asked bluntly if she was married, divorced or engaged.

'No chance! Much too busy,' Kate lied. She suddenly saw the unwelcome image of David Lawrence. She could really do without that dark picture now, she thought, and tried desperately to push away those painful memories of the doctor who had once offered her love. She also refused to think of the time they had lived together. When he had promised her the earth—then left her with nothing but pain.

Now, trying to blot out her thoughts, she stood up from the table, thanked Tilly Marsden for the wonderful tea and then suggested that she should settle into her own flat.

She had a separate entrance, built into a wall at the side of the house. Tilly unlocked the door, then opened it with another flourish, revealing a flight of red-carpeted stairs leading to the floor above.

'Shall I come up with you, me dear? Or would you like to hang on for my son to carry your luggage?' The woman sounded anxious, as if she thought that living in a city had made Kate grow fragile.

'That's kind of you. But I'll manage. Truly.' Kate took the key from her then, seeing a look of disappointment in Tilly's eyes, she regretted her show of independence so added hastily, 'I tell you what. Why don't you help me with the smallest case while I see to the others?'

Relief spread over Tilly's face, and she waited on the bottom step while Kate fetched everything from the car. Then, refusing to be saddled with only one small bag, Tilly helped to haul the heavier things up the stairs to a little landing.

As she looked around Kate felt a sudden and wonderful sense of peace. 'Your son's certainly done a splendid job here, Mrs Marsden,' she said softly.

'He'd be pleased to hear it so why not tell him yourself some time? You're bound to meet him when you go shopping, me dear.'

'Really?'

'If you eat meat, that is. His proper job is running the butcher's on the New Barling estate. Lives over the shop with his wife, Sally.'

Kate smiled. 'I'll also have to tell him I'm sure to be very happy here, Mrs Marsden.'

The woman's face broke into a beaming smile. 'It'll be a pleasure to have you as a lodger, my lovely.' Her voice was warm, and her Devon-blue eyes sparkled with mischief as she added, 'But I thought I asked you to call me Tilly. Everyone else round here does.'

Kate started by stacking books on the shelves Bert Marsden had built. He certainly hadn't wasted an inch of space, she thought, admiring his handiwork as she opened a little door to a miniature bathroom where everything fitted perfectly.

She then went on to the kitchen, putting her meagre stock of dry food into one of the wall cupboards. Here was everything a single woman could possibly need, she thought, glancing at a new gas cooker, a stainless-steel sink with mixer taps, a fridge and masses of worktops. Opening the fridge, she found milk and butter which Tilly must have bought for her. Then she moved on to the bedroom.

Overlooking the village street, it was large and airy with a wardrobe, a chest of drawers and a comfortable double bed. And, thank goodness, a phone placed on a small table beside it, which would save her from having to leap out of bed to take night calls.

Finally she went to the sitting room at the back of the flat. Here was a large open hearth with a portable electric fire as an alternative to logs or coal. Furnished with a sofa and easy chairs, Kate thought the room perfect because it was so homely. It was also beautifully light, with no sign of the poky lattices usually found in country houses. There was just one large picture window, overlooking a walled garden where brambles climbed and daffodils were almost ready to flower. In the far distance she could see Dartmoor, with its stretches of grassland and the craggy tors that could disappear without warning beneath a blanket of mist.

The views were so enticing that she decided to leave the rest of her unpacking and go to the moor before evening came. Grabbing an anorak and pocketing her key, she hurried down the stairs then walked along the village street. As a slight breeze rose out of nowhere, tugging at her light bronze hair, she found herself near the New Barling estate and paused for a moment to look at it.

A sprawl of modern houses was cut through by small avenues. On the edge was a prefab where the surgery was held. Kate would spend most of her time here, but would also take sessions at The Rowans.

After giving New Barling the once-over, she swung towards the moor and didn't stop until she felt springy grass beneath her feet. Pausing to look at the view, she tried to recall the new colleagues she'd met at her interview and wondered what they would be like to work with.

So far she could see little difficulty. Apart from John Smith, perhaps, a junior doctor who'd seemed rather full of himself. With a smile she remembered the way he had tried to flirt with her, taking her arm when Maurice Gilmore had suggested tea in the staff common room at The Rowans.

She had also met Sheila Venables, a middle-aged widow who had set up a Well Woman Clinic in the New Barling surgery, which she ran successfully. She had seemed quite easy to get along with, as had the practice nurses and receptionists she had met briefly.

The only unknown quantity was Ben Alloway, who had been on leave when she was interviewed, and Kate hoped that he would be easy to work with. But she somehow doubted it. When Maurice Gilmore had spoken of the elusive Ben she'd seen the brash young Dr Smith pull a face. Oh, he had covered it hastily with a smile, of course, but not before Kate had gathered that Dr Ben Alloway might be difficult.

Now she noticed the first dark clouds of evening gathering in the sky so she decided to turn back before she got hopelessly lost. Then, suddenly, she saw what she had mistaken for a standing stone walking rapidly towards her.

The man was still carrying his sketch pad, this time tucked beneath one arm. And a whole array of pencils stuck out at various angles from the breast pocket of his grey anorak.

'Hullo, there!' he called.

She wanted to leave but suddenly found that she couldn't move, so she just stood there, staring at him and waiting for those angry eyes to snap at her again.

'So we meet again!' he said, now sounding so friendly that it was difficult to ignore him.

He must be a Grockle, she thought. With the speech of an educated holiday-maker. 'Yes,' she said warily, then added. 'We haven't met before, have we? Apart from earlier on, I mean.'

'No. Why do you ask?'

'Because of the way you looked at me. I thought. . .'

'Oh, that! I'm sorry if I stared. People tell me I do that when I'm preoccupied.'

But that didn't explain the dislike she'd seen in his eyes, did it?

Deciding not to pursue this train of thought, she said, 'Why were you hurrying towards me just now?'

For a moment he looked puzzled. Then that attractive smile spread over his face.

'Oh, please don't look so startled. I'm quite harmless,' he said. 'I just wanted to warn you about the quagmire near here.' He pointed vaguely to a patch of darker earth which had a white signpost stuck into it. 'Even though it's marked, you can't really see it after sunset.'

'Any more than you can see to do your drawing!' She didn't know what on earth had made her say that. It sounded cheeky and provocative. 'Sorry! I don't usually pry. But I just wondered why you bothered to draw when using a camera would be so much easier. Is it because you're an artist?'

He grinned at her. And as a sudden wind tugged at his dark blond hair, spreading it every which way, the dark blue eyes which had held anger only a short time ago now twinkled at her.

'Sometimes I am,' he said enigmatically. 'I'm all sorts of things, really. Interested in the wild flowers one is no longer allowed to pick. Herbs that grow here, too. I'm also a bit of a writer, I suppose. At the moment I'm doing a book on herbal medicine for an obscure publisher whom I wish wasn't quite so unknown.'

Kate was amazed. 'And this is your work?' she asked. 'You actually earn your living doing this?'

Now he was laughing, throwing his head back so that his hair flopped about like a badly made haystack. 'Good grief, no! I just want people to learn more about the very real healing properties hidden in some of our native plants. Also to warn them not to dabble because a few can also be very dangerous.' He looked at her for a moment—weighing her up, she thought. Then he said, 'My real job is more conventional. You see, I'm a doctor.'

Kate couldn't prevent her mouth opening in surprise. Then she said, 'So am I.'

'Here on a well-earned holiday?'

'No. To work. At the twin practice in Lanbury.'

He stared at her with surprise. Then he said slowly, 'So you must be Dr Kate Frinton.'

'Yes—I am,' she said.

Immediately he thrust out his hand, and before she

quite knew how it had happened she felt her fingers being squeezed warmly by his.

'Welcome to Lanbury,' he said. 'I'm Ben Alloway. The doctor who unfortunately missed your interview.'

A moment later spots of rain began to spatter across Kate's face, and she saw him shove his drawing pad into a large pocket of his anorak. Then she felt her arm being gripped firmly by a very strong hand.

'What the hell do you think you're doing?' she said, trying to shake him off.

'Taking you to my car, Dr Frinton. I don't suppose you've brought your own. And I guess you don't know the first thing about the temperamental weather we have here. It's now almost April—when the showers that are supposed to be gentle can actually lash one's skin with hail.'

'But they're supposed to bring May flowers!' she gasped as he hurried her along with scarcely enough time to put her feet down.

'Not here they don't. This is the place where prisoners who are stupid enough to break out of Dartmoor gaol can meet their deaths.'

This silenced her, and for the first time in her life her idyllic picture of Devon vanished.

'So—where are you taking me? After the car, I mean.'

'To Tilly Marsden's, of course. I was told you're renting her flat. Why? Did you think I was trying to kidnap you?'

'Of course not!'

There was a strange sort of comfort in the hand which was holding her arm so firmly, and she suddenly didn't want him to take it away. Then she told herself not to be such a fool. For heaven's sake, what did she think she was doing? Looking for involvement or something?

They reached an old but still serviceable Bentley, and she found herself being pushed into the passenger seat. Then he took the drawing pad out of his pocket and handed it to her.

'Hold this for me, will you?' he said. 'I don't want to crush it more than necessary.'

She took it, trying to resist a strong temptation to look at his work. As he moved into the driving seat, pushing in the ignition key then switching on the engine, he glanced at her and smiled.

'Go on,' he said. 'You have my permission to look. Of course the sketches aren't finished so they may seem dull. They'll be better when I've given them some colour.'

'But they're wonderful as they are!' she exclaimed, riffling through them.

Then she could find nothing further to say because he was now looking steadily at her with a twinkle in those eyes again, and she found that she couldn't look away. She felt as if she were under some kind of spell, and her cheeks grew hot with embarrassment. But still she couldn't move her gaze away from him.

At last he put the car in gear and as they began to climb a steep hill he said softly, 'Who taught you that flattery will get you everywhere, Dr Frinton?'

'I think you're misquoting,' she said breathlessly. 'Isn't it supposed to get you nowhere?'

He gave her a quick glance. Then she saw him shrug. 'Maybe you're right, Doctor. But, tell me, does that mean you have no time for flattery? Because you're too honest, perhaps?'

What a strange thing to say, Kate thought. And she turned to look at him for a moment. All the humour that had been in his face seemed to have disappeared. Now the only expression she could see was a kind of bleakness in those dark blue eyes, and she wondered what was troubling him. But it was fleeting.

By the time they reached her front door it had given way to the smile that intrigued her against her will. Oh, yes, definitely against her will, she told herself as she left the car.

The sudden squall had eased now, turning into a mere few spots of spring rain. So she stood on the pavement as she thanked him for the lift.

'My pleasure,' he said. Then he added, 'Have you found time to buy food yet?'

'No. It's Saturday tomorrow so I'll go shopping then. Dr Gilmore doesn't expect me to start work until next week.'

'But supper—had you thought of that?'

'It's all in hand, thank you. I've decided to eat out. Can you recommend somewhere reasonable?'

'Try the Three Feathers. It's clean and fairly quiet as pubs go. They're also used to serving Grockles!'

She laughed. 'Thanks. I may well do that.'

Just before he drove off he said, 'I often eat there myself so maybe I'll see you again sooner than you think.'

And she was left with the strangest of feelings, moving deep inside her. There was a kind of panic just in case he really did turn up at The Three Feathers.

There was also a feeling of emptiness in case he didn't.

CHAPTER TWO

AFTER passing a small café at the New Barling end of the village, Kate walked to the Three Feathers which was tucked away in a side street near a row of little stone cottages. Refreshed after a shower and wearing a blue cashmere dress with a matching light twill jacket, she felt ready for anything or anyone. But as she saw some of the locals going into the pub she realised that she was terribly overdressed.

Most of the men looked as if they had come straight from work, wearing tatty jeans and T-shirts. And the few women she saw, trailing after them, looked far too young to be here. But she was hungry so, even though she might look like a prize Grockle, she walked in with her head held high.

A quiet place, Ben Alloway had said. As a burst of loud chatter met her from a crowd leaning against the bar she decided that he must be deaf. And used to serving Grockles? The moment she was spotted the voices died instantly, and she met an invisible barrier of hostility as some of the men began to eye her. At that point she thought the herb-loving doctor must also be mad.

Then a male voice with a thick Devon burr called out loudly, 'Evenin', miss! Wot'll you be wanting?'

The man was standing behind the bar in front of a row of Optics. Must be the landlord, Kate thought, giving him a smile and waiting for him to smile back.

19

When he didn't she walked steadily towards him and asked, 'You serve meals here?'

'We do.' He frowned. 'Passing through, are you, miss?'

'No. I live here now. And it's Doctor—not Miss.'

If she had announced that he was the winner of the National Lottery she couldn't have made a greater impression. The man immediately straightened up and gave her a look bordering on reverence as a little smile began to pull at the corners of his mouth.

'Well, I never!' he said. 'We'd heard there was to be a new one, but I didn't expect a doctor straight from Hollywood!'

'Really?' Kate gave him a professional smile which she hoped was also friendly. 'Perhaps I should warn you that doctors in films don't know the first thing about illness. A real doctor is far more reliable. So just remember that if you ever come to me as a patient, will you?'

The man looked taken aback for a moment, then obviously realised that she was only teasing so he grinned at her. 'Well said!' he murmured, his voice now spiced with admiration. 'But somehow I don't think that'll happen. Old Gilmore at The Rowans is my doc, and I s'pose you'll be at New Barling.'

'Not all the time. I believe the doctors share the two practices so I'll be working at The Rowans sometimes.'

'But mainly at New Barling?'

'Probably.'

'That's great!' another voice chimed in. This belonged to a young man, standing at the end of the bar. He looked like some sort of labourer, and after grinning cheerfully at Kate he slipped one arm round a slender, pale-looking girl in jeans and a flimsy blouse who seemed to have eyes for no one but him. 'Maisie and I've just got wed. Moved from Barnstable to the new estate here. But we haven't got round to finding a doctor yet.'

The girl he called Maisie gave Kate such a sweet smile that she felt her heart melting. She was like a trusting child, and was so thin that Kate wouldn't have been surprised if a sudden gust of wind had blown her away. She wondered when the girl had last eaten and what sort of food she served to her new husband. If, indeed, she ever gave him a hot meal.

Then the girl said shyly, 'P'raps we could both be on your list, Doctor. We're Maisie and Joe Brown.'

Her first patients? Hardly. Kate remembered the strict rota in her Midlands practice where the last in never had the first choice. 'We'll have to see,' she said. 'I can't promise anything, but you could always ask for me when you register, I suppose.'

'So who do we say we want?'

'Dr Frinton. Now, if you'll excuse me, I really must order something to eat. Since I got to Devon all I've had is thunder and lightning!'

The landlord laughed. 'That'll be at Tilly Marsden's place, I'll be bound!' He gave her a beaming smile and said, 'I'm George Dowling, by the way. So, what would you like for your supper?'

Twenty minutes later Kate was eating fish and chips served by George's wife, who introduced herself as Helen. Sitting at a table in a small dining extension, which still gave her a view of the door, she watched the group by the bar who were chatting loudly to each other again.

Occasionally some of them turned to look at her, but now they seemed friendly so she considered that she had passed the Grockle test. If she could win over her new patients as easily then working in Lanbury would be just fine.

A moment later the door opened to let someone in. Kate looked up, half expecting to see Ben Alloway, and tried to still a heart that was thudding. Then she felt a ridiculous disappointment when she saw John Smith walk to the bar.

'Evenin', Doc!' George Dowling greeted him with a cheerful grin. 'Come looking for your new partner, have you? She's over there.'

There was no escape so Kate tried to make the best of it when John brought a pint glass to her table.

'Hello, there! Mind if I join you?' he asked.

She wanted to ignore him. She just wasn't in the mood for his brand of dalliance. Yet she didn't want to risk discourtesy at the start of her new job so she inclined her head as graciously as she could and said, 'Help yourself! It's a free country.'

After giving her a curious stare, as if he had caught a hint of what she really felt, he sat opposite her and smiled. 'I thought I might find you here,' he said.

'Oh? Were you looking for me?'

'Well—yes,' he admitted. 'I called at your flat and found you'd gone out, then Tilly Marsden told me you might be here.'

'What did you want?'

'Oh, nothing really important. Just to talk about rosters and so on.'

Kate stared blankly at him. She'd thought that work

would be the last thing on his mind. That on a Friday night he'd be whooping it up with some girl or other.

'But I haven't seen a roster yet. Dr Gilmore suggested I wait until Monday. Why, I haven't even seen *him* yet!'

'No, well. . .but before you do there's something I ought to tell you. To—warn you about, I suppose.'

Kate felt herself bridling. 'What on earth do you mean, Dr Smith?'

He began to look uncomfortable, but that didn't stop him from saying, 'If the kind of treatment the old man gives you is anything like the way he deals with me then you'll soon find yourself being watched. All the time.'

'So I should hope! Any senior partner has the right to examine what other doctors are doing. Especially if they're new to the practice. In fact, it's his duty, isn't it?'

His face flushed. 'So you won't mind working under the Gestapo?'

'Don't be so ridiculous! I've been practising medicine for some years, and never once have I felt I was being policed. In fact, I've always been grateful for any help offered.' Kate glanced at him and saw his brown eyes suddenly smoulder with a kind of hurt. Deciding that she'd probably been too hard on him, she said more gently, 'Is this your first real experience of hands-on medicine?'

'Not exactly. I spent a year in a Berkshire practice after I qualified as a GP.'

'Only one year? So what happened?'

He looked away from her, ran nervous hands through curly dark brown hair then said slowly, 'I. . .er. . .well, I left.'

Before he could face a charge of negligence? Maybe

something worse? Kate really didn't want to know, but
felt herself softening towards this young man who had
appeared so self-important when she'd first met him.
Now he seemed different. And, sensing a kind of desperation in him, she suddenly wanted to help, even though
she felt reluctant.

'Like to talk about it?' she suggested.

'Er—not really. One day, perhaps. For now, it's
enough to say I got involved with a girl and certain
people objected.'

'With a *patient*?'

'Oh, no! Nothing like that.'

Thank God for that, Kate thought, then wondered who
the people objecting to a love affair could possibly be in
these enlightened days. But it was really none of her
business, she told herself, and speared a piece of fish,
determined to finish her meal before it congealed on
the plate.

Here she was unlucky for the door opened again and
suddenly Ben Alloway was there, smiling as he walked
towards her. But when he caught sight of John Smith he
hesitated, then frowned.

'I didn't realise you two knew each other,' he said
stiffly. 'So, if you'll excuse me, I'll leave you to it.'

He was already turning away when Kate said, 'There's
no need. Dr Smith was just going.' She fixed John with
a severe stare and added, '*Weren't you?*'

'Of course.' Leaving his drink on the table, John
slipped smoothly out of his chair and sauntered towards
the door as if he hadn't a care in the world.

When he had gone Ben Alloway sank into the chair
and Kate said, 'Let's get one thing straight before we

start working together, shall we? I most certainly don't know Dr Smith. Nor does he know me. We met after my interview, that's all.'

Ben gave her a puzzled look. 'So what was he doing here?'

'Having a drink, maybe?' She indicated the glass still half-full of beer. 'So perhaps you'd be good enough to tell me why he was so willing to leave the moment you appeared. Also why you're here. Looking for me, were you?'

'You sound annoyed.'

'Do I? Well, maybe I am. I don't like being spied on any more than Dr Smith does.'

Ben Alloway frowned. 'Is that what he told you?'

Kate stayed silent for a moment, not wanting to indulge in idle chatter—especially about a colleague. But when she saw a touch of anxiety in Ben's eyes she knew without being told that this was not just a random question.

'Yes, that's more or less when he said,' she murmured.

'And he also warned you, I suppose.'

'Ye-s. But I didn't take much notice. I happen to believe that doctors should help each other, and if that entails keeping watch over a new member of staff then so be it.'

Ben immediately relaxed and his anxiety, which she now realised must have been for her, disappeared. Then he smiled at her with amusement and said quietly, 'You're nothing if not direct.'

'Without being abrasive, I hope.'

His deep blue eyes were now dancing with hidden laughter, and she smiled back at him as he said, 'Oh, never that! You're the kind of doctor I'm certain will be a joy to work with.'

For a moment she was held captive by the warmth of his glance and wanted to stay here for ever just looking at him, as if she were in some delicious kind of dream.

Then this impossible dream was shattered by a sudden commotion near the bar, and the landlord was calling her name. When he caught sight of Ben he said, 'Perhaps this is something you should both deal with. 'Tis this young lass here. She seems to have collapsed.'

Ben took in the scene immediately and told Kate to go to the girl while he fetched his medical bag from his car. Then he rushed through the open door like a gust of moorland wind.

After asking people to stand back, Kate saw Joe Brown kneeling beside his wife who was slumped in an awkward sitting position. She watched him smoothing the girl's cheeks with his labourer's hands which had grown as gentle as swansdown, and heard him saying, 'Maisie, love! Wake up! For God's sake, don't go to sleep on me now.'

Sleep, he called it, and Kate wondered why. Did she suffer from a disorder like sleep apnoea, where breathing ceased for a short while before being resumed naturally? This could be very frightening to those watching and sometimes indicated other more serious conditions, such as obstruction of the airways. But somehow Kate didn't think so in Masie's case as she now seemed to be breathing normally again. 'It looks to me as if your wife has fainted,' she said, then asked, 'Has this sort of thing happened to her before?'

'Quite often,' Joe said, his voice husky with fear.

After undoing the top button of the girl's blouse to find a pulse in her neck and lifting her eyelids to look at the pupils—and finding nothing spectacular there—Kate gently laid Maisie flat on her back. A man offered his jacket as a pillow but Kate refused to take it.

'She must lie level like this,' she said.

'But if she's fainted shouldn't her head be between her knees?' a woman asked, and Kate tried not to snap as she said, 'Not these days.'

'I should have thought that's the best treatment, Doc,' someone else said. 'My gran always told me. . .'

Kate looked up momentarily, saw a girl as young as Maisie staring at her with an expression of sheer doom and gave her a smile. 'Please!' she murmured. 'I know what I'm doing so just trust me, will you?'

Glad that she had been here when the girl had collapsed, Kate shuddered to think what these people might have done with her when their knowledge of first aid seemed to be based on old wives' tales.

'She must have air,' Kate went on in a low voice as everyone stared in silence. Placing her hand gently beneath Maisie's chin, she pushed it upwards to make sure there was a clear passage into the throat.

Although Maisie Brown had temporarily lost the use of her legs, she had not yet slipped into complete unconsciousness. Then Kate saw her eyelids flicker, and gave a sigh of relief as Maisie took in a shuddering breath.

'Bring me a glass of water, will you?' she called out to no one in particular. Putting one arm around the girl, she lifted her a little and supported her back against her own body. The thin hands were deathly cold, but a tinge of colour was now coming into her pale cheeks.

'Here y'are, Doc!' George Dowling handed Kate a glass of water which she held to Maisie's lips, encouraging her to sip slowly.

At last Ben returned, knelt down beside the girl and checked the pulse in one wrist, timing the beat against a watch. Kate studied him closely, feeling happier when she saw how caring he seemed.

'I need to examine her more thoroughly. I really don't like her colour.' He spoke softly to Kate then looked up at George Dowling, who was hovering at the front of the crowd, and said, 'Can we take her somewhere more comfortable so that I can examine her properly? Preferably without an audience!'

Kate thought his words might put a few backs up, but they didn't. It seemed that the villagers were genuinely fond of the man whom some of them were now calling 'Dr Ben', and she caught amusement on their faces as one of the men said to her, 'Shy as a violet is our dear doc. Just remember that when you're working with him, miss. Er—sorry, I mean Dr Frinton.'

Kate grinned at the man as George led the way to a room marked PRIVATE at the back of the pub. Then Ben carried Maisie carefully through the door, while Kate followed with the new husband who now looked a little more cheerful.

Ben lowered Maisie onto a sofa. 'She's no heavier that a couple of feathers,' he breathed to Kate. 'I've never seen her before. Do you know who her doctor is?'

'She and her husband haven't been here long. They're Joe and Maisie Brown. Live in New Barling, they told me, but haven't registered with a GP yet.'

Joe Brown heard this and after clearing his throat

nervously he said, 'We hoped Dr Frinton would take us on. But she thought that might be difficult.'

Ben raised enquiring eyebrows at Kate and she said hastily, 'I don't yet know if you have a strict rota system.'

'We haven't. So, if you're willing. . .'

'I am. Of course.'

'There you are, you see!' Ben said to Joe. 'It's really quite simple. But, of course, if at any time you yourself would rather see a man then there are three of us to choose from. All ready to do our best for you.'

He then focused that wonderful smile on the pair of newly-weds, and Kate saw the man relaxing under the charisma that surrounded this most intriguing of doctors. How does he do it? she asked herself. Then she decided that it was a gift he must have been born with.

A moment later, as George tactfully left them and went back to the bar, Ben set about examining Maisie more thoroughly, using his stethoscope to sound every inch of her chest. Then he invited Kate to use it, which she did.

'As clear as a bell,' she said, handing the instrument to Ben when she'd finished.

The small touch of colour in the girl's cheeks was now fading again. Kate wasn't happy about her so she flipped down one of her lower eyelids, looking for a more healthy colour there. But she found only a pale wash of pink.

Straightening up, she asked Joe Brown, 'When did your wife last eat?'

The young man was confused. 'I don't really know, Doc. I'm a brickie, working on those extra houses going up in the new estate. So I'm out all day, see. Take sandwiches with me.'

'Do you eat together when you come home?'

'Of course. We always have our supper then.'

'A good hot meal?'

'Oh, yes. Maisie's a great cook. Did it at school, see? Stew is her favourite.'

'And tonight?'

'Well, we haven't got round to it yet. It being Friday, I thought I'd treat her to a drink first. But we stayed longer than we meant to. You know how it is.'

Kate did. She also knew that this wasn't the whole story, and suspected that once Joe hurried off with his sandwiches in the morning Maisie forgot all about food for herself. But why? Vanity? Or was there some other hidden agenda here?

At last she said, 'I think your wife could do with some iron tablets, Joe. But before I prescribe them I'd like her to have a blood test.' She turned to Ben. 'What arrangements are there for this at the surgery?'

'Simple! Once you've taken the blood Mary Kolinski, one of our practice nurses, will send it off for testing. She'll even do the whole thing herself if you let her know what tests you need. How about Monday? She's assisting at New Barling in the morning. If it's done first off the sample can be sent immediately by courier to Plymouth or Exeter.'

'Great! So I'll register Maisie at the same time.' Kate looked at Joe. 'Could you get time off to bring your wife in?'

'Er—sure!' The man sounded doubtful, then added, 'We haven't got round to buying a car yet.'

'Don't worry, lad!' Ben said. 'I'll pick her up myself. Take her back home again, if need be.'

'Oh, but—we don't want to be a nuisance, sir. A mate

drives me to work. He can take Maisie to the surgery first.'

'But how about her getting back?'

'It's not that far. She likes a walk and she'll be better by then, won't she?'

'I expect so. But it wouldn't be any trouble for me to do it.'

'No, thanks, Doctor. We can manage. Really.'

So—Ben was not only charismatic but kind, Kate thought. Then she wondered if she would be able to keep her head when she worked with him. But, suddenly impatient with her thoughts, she told herself severely to get rid of these ridiculous feelings. She really would have to stop them rising in her whenever he was near. It would be extremely hard, she realised. But, whatever happened, she must keep her relationship with him purely professional.

'Did you come here by car?' Ben asked Kate.

Managing at last to blank out her disturbing thoughts, she said, 'No, I walked.'

He turned to Joe Brown. 'And I suppose you and your wife walked too?'

'Yes. But I guess she's not well enough to walk back, is she? So we'll ask someone for a lift.'

'No need. I'll take you both home. Some food, followed by a good night's sleep, is what she needs at the moment. So come with me, will you?'

Kate began to wander back to the bar but Ben called after her, wanting to know what she thought she was doing.

'Just going to thank the landlord and pay for my meal. Then I'll be on my way home.'

'Thank him and pay, by all means. But then you'll be coming with me. After all, Mrs Brown is your patient, isn't she?'

The house on the new estate was shrouded in darkness, and by the light of a streetlamp Kate saw that the front garden was still full of builders' rubble. Hardly a warm welcome for the newly married couple, she thought, and only hoped that the house would be less bleak inside.

'Mind you don't trip on all that uneven ground,' Joe warned, producing a key and flinging the front door wide so that Ben, who was supporting Maisie, could walk inside with her.

Then they all moved across a small hallway to a living room. Here things seemed a little better for a gas fire was burning on a low setting, with two fairly new easy chairs drawn up to it. Against a wall along one side of the room was a rather tattered-looking couch, with a pink blanket rumpled on it. As if Maisie had been resting there, before being taken to the pub, Kate thought.

Looking swiftly around, she saw that there wasn't much else in the way of furniture and for the first time she realised how poverty-stricken the place really was.

As Ben helped Maisie onto the couch Joe said, 'We're not really straight yet, Doctor. But the place is as clean as a new pin. My Maisie's so house-proud—she spends ages working on it.'

'Is it yours, or do you rent it?' Ben asked, and Kate saw Joe's face flush with embarrassment.

'It's rented,' he admitted. 'The council owns most of these properties. But one day we hope to have a place of our own. When we've saved enough, that is.'

Kate asked if she could go to the kitchen. 'I think a few sweet biscuits would be the best thing for your wife at the moment,' she said. 'A hot drink, too, like tea or cocoa. Shall I see to it?'

'Oh, thanks a lot, Doctor. It's the room at the end of the hall.'

In a small and compact kitchen Kate found plenty of cupboards, but there was precious little food in any of them. However, she discovered three digestive biscuits in a tin, half a carton of milk in a fridge that was almost empty and a packet of sweetened drinking chocolate, needing only the addition of hot water. After putting the powder into a mug she filled it up with water from an electric kettle and stirred the mixture vigorously. Then, putting two of the biscuits on a small plate, she took it all to the living room.

'Here you go,' she said, balancing the plate on one arm of the sofa and handing over the mug. When she saw Maisie's cold fingers begin to tremble she helped the girl to lift it to her lips. 'I've made this with water,' she said. 'But later I'd like you to drink some milk. Is there anyone who can do some shopping for you?'

Maisie stared at her, her eyes listless. 'I can manage,' she said. 'There's a shop on the estate.'

But no money to spend in it, Kate thought, and wondered how she could help this frail girl without offending her.

Ben also seemed to realise the difficulty, and managed the issue with much more tact than she could ever have done. 'I expect you're paid weekly, aren't you?' he said to Joe. 'On Mondays too, I should imagine, so that the gaffer makes sure you get into work.'

'That's right. The boss is funny that way. In my last place we got our money on Fridays. But in New Barling no such luck.'

'Then let me pay for a few groceries, will you?'

'Oh, no, that won't do at all.'

'Then I'll buy them myself and bring them over.'

'But. . .'

Ben's eyes suddenly snapped with determination. 'Don't argue with me, man! You can pay me back when you're more settled here. I won't take no for an answer so you may as well give in.'

Kate saw Ben's mouth lifting into that attractive smile, and it seemed that Joe couldn't resist it any more than she had been able to when they'd first met on Dartmoor.

'OK, Doc, you win!' the young man said as he saw them both out of the sad little house. 'But I'll pay you back, I promise!'

'No need to hurry, lad. I won't starve while I'm waiting.'

As Ben drove Kate to her flat he said, 'Did you detect anything else, apart from possible anaemia?'

'Well, yes,' she admitted. 'I have a strong feeling that our sweet young bride is already pregnant.'

He chuckled softly. 'Something only a woman would know?'

'Not really. When I watched you examining her chest I saw a tell-tale blue ring around the areolae of her breasts.'

'Did you, indeed? I'm damned if I noticed it.'

'Well, you wouldn't necessarily, would you? You were concentrating on what might be happening in her lungs.'

'And they seemed perfectly healthy, thank God.'

When they drew up in front of Tilly Marsden's house

Kate invited Ben in for coffee. But he refused, saying that he must get back to his own house.

She looked at him enquiringly, waiting for him to tell her where it was. When he didn't she wasn't entirely surprised for, now she came to think of it, she really didn't know anything about him or his private life. And, as far as she could see, he was content to leave it that way.

Apart from the work he was doing for an obscure publisher, and the fact that he visited the Three Feathers, he was a complete mystery. For all she knew he could be married with a family of growing children.

This thought suddenly brought her a strange feeling of sadness. But she pushed it aside as she hurried upstairs, telling herself not to be such a fool.

CHAPTER THREE

THE next morning Kate woke early, feeling fresh despite her long drive to Devon. Even niggling worries over her first patient, thrust at her unexpectedly in the Three Feathers the previous night, hadn't disturbed her sleep. Today was Saturday so she decided on a quick shower, followed by a morning's shopping. She might even have time for coffee in that café she'd seen on her way to the pub, she thought.

But all these plans went awry. The moment she'd dressed in leggings and pullover her phone rang. Curious, sure that no one knew her number yet, she snatched up the receiver and heard a man ask, 'So how are you feeling this morning?'

'I think you must have a wrong number,' she said.

There was a low chuckle. 'I take it that I'm speaking to Dr Frinton?'

'You are. But I'm sorry, I don't know who. . .'

'That's not surprising, my dear. The last time we spoke was at your interview.'

'Dr Gilmore!' she exclaimed. 'I'm so sorry. I should have recognised you.'

'Without the face?' He laughed again. 'I'm often told that my wrinkles don't really match my voice because, apparently, I sound surprisingly youthful!'

Kate could find nothing to say. At the interview Maurice Gilmore had been very much the boss in charge.

Pleasant and friendly, but certainly not bordering on the flippant like this. Was this a taste of the camaraderie she'd often longed for in her last practice but had never found?

At last she said, 'What can I do for you, Doctor?'

'I know I shouldn't be taking up your free time like this, but I wondered how you were finding things and also if you'd like to come to The Rowans and take a cup of coffee with me.'

Kate smiled to herself. Did one actually 'take' coffee these days? He sounded so sweet and old-fashioned that she immediately imagined him in frock coat and top hat, like an etching she'd once seen of the famous Dr Barnardo.

'I'd love to. When?'

'Could you manage this morning? Then we can discuss your hours and so on for the coming week.'

'Fine! I'll look forward to it.'

So much for breakfast and shopping, she thought as she hastily brushed her tousled bronze hair and slapped a touch of make-up on her face. But it couldn't be helped. Hopefully she would find somewhere still open when she left The Rowans—if not in Lanbury or the new estate then in the nearest town, which was Tanwyth.

Hurrying into the kitchen, she drank some of the milk Tilly had provided then shrugged herself into an anorak. Making sure that she had her keys, she slung the straps of her bag over her shoulder and darted downstairs. A moment later she was driving through the village in the opposite direction from New Barling. After climbing a number of hills, bordered by high hedges, she eventually reached The Rowans—a large square house of mellowed bricks, covered in bright red creeper.

When she'd first seen it she'd imagined it as Maurice Gilmore's private castle. Quietly gracious, it made a wonderful setting for a man who seemed both powerful and gentle. Very human too. For when they'd talked together after her interview she'd known that she was in the presence of a doctor who had never once lost sight of his patients as individuals.

Now looking forward to seeing him again, Kate left her car on a gravelled drive, walked up some well-worn stone steps and then pulled at an old-fashioned bell and waited.

The door was opened by Mrs Penright, the middle-aged housekeeper whom Kate had met previously. Maurice Gilmore had spoken of her as Sarah, explaining with a wicked twinkle in his blue eyes that she came from 'the distant land of Cornwall' and had only considered moving to Devon when her husband died.

'Can you imagine the upheaval there was, coming to a "foreign country" like this?' he'd said, and Kate had found his question strange. But, since learning about Grockles from Tilly Marsden, it at last made sense.

'Good morning, Doctor.' The merest flicker of a smile touched Sarah Penright's face, doing nothing to disguise the suspicion in her dark brown eyes which were now staring at Kate as if she had come from the moon. 'Dr Gilmore is in the drawing room on the first landing so perhaps you'd like to go up while I see to the coffee he ordered.'

Kate thanked her and mounted elegant stairs, carpeted in grey Axminster. As she reached the landing a door opened, and she stood quite still as her new senior partner walked towards her. She thought how distinguished he looked. Although dressed casually, his grey trousers were beautifully pressed and his dark blue cashmere sweater looked as if it had come straight from Harrods.

For a moment she felt quite daunted, and wished that she hadn't jumped into the first clothes she could find. Her anorak positively screamed in this dignified place— to say nothing of black leggings, topped by a garish multicoloured pullover.

'So you remembered where I live and didn't get lost!'

As he smiled Kate found it hard to believe that he was near retirement. Never had grey hair looked so youthful, and the laughter dancing in his eyes made her feel so at home that she hoped he would never stop working.

'How could I forget?' she said, completely at ease with him as he offered her a chair then sat opposite her. 'I think I'll always remember the tea and cakes you gave us all after my interview.'

'Really? The occasion was rather stiff, I thought. A sort of business tea in that formal room downstairs which my colleagues fondly call the staff barracks!' He laughed softly. 'I hope this little get-together will be less starchy. It's meant to give you confidence for Monday, my dear. But I gather you've already acquired your first patient!'

Surprised, she asked, 'How did you know?'

'Ben Alloway phoned me late last night. Told me you'd already met. I also gather he thinks your work here will be more than just adequate.'

'That's kind of him.' Kate tried to control a flush, spreading over her cheeks.

'Not kind, Doctor. Ben never uses words he doesn't really mean, as you'll soon find.'

Sarah Penright came in at that moment, setting a tray of coffee and biscuits on a small table. 'This room needs a bit of warmth,' she said, and switched on a large electric fire which stood in a hearth beneath an ornate mantelpiece.

After pouring coffee into two bone china cups, she suggested that both doctors should help themselves to sugar and cream, then left. But not before giving Kate another highly suspicious glance, which amused her.

'Does she always stare at strangers like that?' Kate asked impulsively.

Maurice Gilmore's face filled with amusement. 'Always! The moment I took old Sarah on she regarded herself as my personal bodyguard. Not that I often need one, of course. But I must say it comes in useful sometimes. Especially if she has to rescue me from trouble.'

'Really?' Kate couldn't imagine him in any kind of trouble. He seemed much too dignified and powerful.

'You find that hard to believe?' Kate nodded. 'Well, then, for your own good I'd better remind you that we live in difficult times. The age of illegal drugs, my dear, where every doctor is at risk from attacks of all kinds. Where some people use knives and guns without a second thought.'

'*Here*? In this quiet place?'

'Yes, even here. The innocence we once knew in Lanbury has passed. I'm sad to say that the change affects all of us.'

'Have you ever been threatened?'

'Yes, but only once. And only because I was foolish enough to open my front door at night without using the chain. Some time after my last patient had left the bell rang. Thinking that some friend had called, I answered the door before Sarah had a chance. The next thing I knew some young man I'd never seen before was grabbing at my jacket and brandishing a knife.'

'How frightening!'

'It was. Luckily Sarah appeared almost at once. She was wonderful! Facing the man like a tiger, she shouted at him, then grabbed his sleeve and shook the knife from his hand. After that she pulled him inside and shoved him into a chair.' Maurice chuckled. 'He was so startled that he just sat there as she glared at him. Then she picked up the knife and pointed it at him while she told me to call the police.'

Kate was appalled. 'So what happened after that?'

'Two officers arrived, charged the man with unlawful entry—or some such thing—and took him away. He's still inside, I believe. Doing time for other offences too. All connected with drugs.'

'And you'd never seen him before?'

'No. He turned out to be a young tearaway from Exeter, breaking into surgeries on the off chance of finding drugs.' Maurice sighed. 'So you see what doctors are up against, even in a charming place like Lanbury.'

'And here was I thinking that I'd left all that sort of thing behind in the Midlands!'

'I hope I haven't put you off, my dear. It doesn't often happen here, I promise you.' He sipped his coffee thoughtfully, then said, 'Now, shall we get down to sorting out your duties?'

'That's fine by me. Do you want me to take notes while you talk?'

'I shouldn't bother. When I've explained everything

I'll give you a file to take home, then you can go through
it at your leisure.'

It was over two hours before Kate left The Rowans with
a file, containing lists of patients allocated to her, information about the hours she would work and a note on
the unique way records were kept. After these were dupli-
cated by the secretaries a copy was left in both surgeries
so that patients could visit either. As Kate already knew
she would spend most of her time at New Barling with
Sheila Venables and John Smith, occasionally sitting at
The Rowans which was run by Maurice and Ben.

The schedule was heavy but manageable, she thought,
with morning and evening sessions held simultaneously
at both practices. Saturday mornings were kept free for
emergencies, and most afternoons were earmarked for
home visits. On Wednesday evenings she was expected
to assist Sheila Venables with the Well Woman Clinic
if the numbers were too great for one doctor.

As for night duties, she considered that she had got
off lightly for the roster was shared with a surgery in
Little Medington, a small village five miles from
Lanbury.

There were also regular practice meetings held at The
Rowans so that the doctors could discuss any difficulties
they'd come across. It seemed like an extra burden but
Kate welcomed it. This way everyone could keep in
touch, working closely as a team.

Finally she learnt that cases needing urgent surgery
were sent to hospitals in Plymouth and Exeter but that
others who needed only minor operations were referred

to Much Willborough, a village which still held onto its cottage hospital.

Arriving back at her flat, Kate put the file away, picked up a large holdall she had brought from the Midlands and hurried downstairs again. She was about to walk along the village street when she saw Tilly Marsden, waving through a window. A moment later the woman appeared at her front door.

'Did you want me?' Kate called.

'You going shopping, Doctor?'

'That's right. Can I get you anything?'

Tilly walked down her garden path and leant on the little iron gate. 'No, thanks, me dear. Just thought I'd warn you about the shops round here. There's only a fish and chip take-away and the general store at the end of the main street, but that shuts on Saturday afternoons.'

Kate looked at her watch, saw that it was already well after midday and frowned. 'So, what about New Barling?'

Tilly shrugged. 'The mini-market there stays open all hours, but there's not much choice. Apart from that, there's only the butcher's my Bert runs.'

'And the shops in Tanwyth? Do they close early?'

'No, you'll be all right there. Plenty of parking space, too.'

'Tanwyth it is, then.' Kate turned to go to her car, then said, 'Like to come with me?'

'That's kind of you, but I'm waiting for Bert. He always brings me a nice cut of steak for Sunday.'

'Right, then. See you later. You're sure there's nothing you want?'

'Well, if you happen to pass a newsagent there's a magazine I'd like. The store here doesn't keep it.'

'Then I'll get it. Just tell me what its called.'

'*Magic of Our Time*'.

Kate smiled. 'So you're a closet conjurer, are you?'

Tilly's face flushed with embarrassment. 'Not exactly,' she said, then admitted reluctantly, 'It's all about those vibrations supposed to be in the earth. A bit hush-hush, really. Bert says I'm mad to dabble with it but I really enjoy it so why shouldn't I indulge myself?'

Kate looked at this ordinary, everyday sort of woman with new eyes. 'You mean the healing power some people believe exists in standing stones, and so on?' she asked in amazement.

'Yes, among other things. I've joined a club that used to meet in the parish hall, but the vicar objected. Said it was ungodly, or some such nonsense. So now we get together in one another's houses every week.' Tilly looked at her curiously for a moment, then asked, 'Would you like to join us one evening?'

Kate could just imagine what her colleagues would say if she did! 'Thanks for the invite, Tilly, but I don't think I'll have much spare time once I start work.'

'No, well. It was just a thought, being as how you don't know many folk yet.'

Kate left it at that, but the idea of her landlady going in for earth mysteries like this kept her amused all the way to Tanwyth.

She found a space in a car park on the edge of the town and fed a meter for two hours, hoping that it would be long enough. Then, slinging the straps of her bag over one shoulder, she picked up the holdall and made her way to the top of a steep hill where shops lined each side of the street. She had seen Tanwyth only rarely as a child because her holidays had been spent in Exmouth, but she remembered it as being quaint and utterly charming.

Going through an archway that seemed to be keeping a benign watch over the town, she paused for a moment and drank in the atmosphere. The view was so unexpected. Different in a way she couldn't really define. There was a special kind of magic about it. The crowds doing their weekend shopping seemed so carefree. Smiling and chatting to each other, even though half of them probably didn't really know the people they spoke to, they looked as if they had all the time in the world.

Standing there and absorbing everything, Kate realised that she must look like a lost soul. Especially when a very large middle-aged man, wearing long black robes and a dog collar, asked her if he could help.

She immediately came out of her dream and smiled at him. 'Not really, but thank you all the same. I'm just shopping,' she said, then asked, 'Where is your church? I'd like to visit it.'

The man laughed. 'I'm not really a vicar,' he said, looking about furtively as he fingered a large gold cross, resting on his chest. 'This is just fancy dress, I'm afraid. On Fridays people who live here are encouraged to wear any costume they like. It's a long-standing tradition, you see.'

'But today is Saturday!'

He grinned. 'I know. But it's fun, looking like a vicar, especially when it brings me respect. I can never bear to take these things off.'

Kate smiled back at him, thinking that this sort of thing could only happen in a place like Tanwyth. 'Does your wife dress up too?'

'I'm afraid I've never had one,' he said, turning solemn. 'I live alone. In a caravan. Granted, some people think I'm mad not having a proper house. But, believe me, I wouldn't live any differently.'

'So, do you tow it by car when you move on?'

'Never had a car either. A horse does me. But I don't even have that since poor Meg died. Now I just stay put.'

'So, if you're not a real cleric, what do you do?'

'To earn a living, you mean? Not much these days. But I get by so don't you go worrying over me, lassie.'

Kate found all this difficult to believe. The man seemed so cultured, his speech sounding highly educated. Yet he lived like a vagrant, probably existing on next to nothing. Then she recalled other well-read people she'd come across who actually preferred this way of life.

She made one last attempt to fit this strange man into a suitable category and asked, 'You're a Romany?'

'Er—maybe. Long ago I was told my granny was, but I don't remember her.' He took in a breath, studying Kate with obvious admiration dancing in a pair of very dark eyes. Then he said, 'And you, miss? You live near here?'

'Quite near. I'm a doctor in New Barling.'

'Is that so? Well, I never! So, how do I address you?' he asked with an amusing kind of old-world charm.

'As Dr Frinton—if you want to be polite.'

The man went on staring at her for a while, those gypsy eyes shining with admiration—which made Kate uncomfortable. Then, without any warning, he turned away and left.

She was intrigued. And even more so when the man came to a sudden halt and said, 'Sorry, Doctor!'

She thought he was speaking to her again. But as she watched him stand back respectfully to let another man pass she realised that he was apologising to him. Then she suddenly found herself facing Ben Alloway.

And there it was again—the almost tangible charisma which seemed to surround the man. For a moment she felt her heartbeat quicken and tried to control the excitement rising in her. This was something she could very definitely do without, she told herself, appalled by her reaction. Just looking at him almost destroyed her. As if she were some vulnerable teenager, she thought irritably.

'Good morning!' he said, sounding unexpectedly stiff and formal.

'I'm shopping,' she faltered, feeling suddenly nervous.

'So I see.' He frowned, then added stiffly, 'Can I take you round the town, or do you already know it?'

'Only a little. From my childhood days.' His frown deepened, as if he resented her being here, and her nervousness increased until words tumbled from her in a rush. 'I need to buy food. Lots of it. And things to brighten up my flat too. Oh, and, yes, I must find a newsagent for Tilly.' She heard herself going on in this senseless way, tried to control herself and ended by asking lamely, 'Where's the best place for all this?'

He stared at her silently, wondering why on earth she was talking in this jumbled way. And he cursed himself for offering to take her around the town. What the devil was he thinking of? The last thing he needed was to spend time with her socially. He'd told himself that when he'd first met her.

But it hadn't stopped him going to the Three Feathers, had it? Pretending to himself that he wasn't really looking for her. Denying that he'd felt a stab of something utterly wonderful when they'd met on the moor.

When he'd seen her with John Smith last night he had felt resentment deep inside. He'd wanted to get rid of the wretched man so that he could have her all to himself—even though he knew this was the last thing he should wish for. He couldn't deal with it.

All those childish feelings had fled when Maisie Brown fainted. Afterwards he'd found working with Kate so natural and easy that he'd no longer been afraid for himself.

Now all he felt was a surge of anger because once again he'd been tempted to overstep the mark.

Kate looked at him, seeing his anger, and suddenly found that she couldn't look away from him. And as her gaze locked with his she realised that he was in some kind of private dream. But he wasn't seeing a pleasant image, she thought. Now a kind of sadness was flitting over his face, and it seemed to be torturing him.

But at last the spell broke and he frowned, before saying gruffly, 'At the bottom of this hill you'll find a superstore. And before that there are lots of newsagents.'

'Thanks,' she said shortly. Annoyed by his sudden coolness, she turned away to walk down the hill.

But a moment later she felt a hand on her arm as he said, 'I'm sorry. I didn't mean to fob you off like that. It's just that. . .well, I was thinking of something else.

Just let me get rid of my own shopping, and I'll come with you.'

For the first time she noticed that he was carrying a bag, stuffed full of groceries. 'Thanks,' she said crisply, 'but I don't want to delay you.'

'You won't. Just wait a second and I'll be with you.' He darted into a greengrocer's shop, then reappeared empty-handed. 'I know them in there, and they're used to looking after my things when I find something better to do. If you're anything like me you probably find shopping alone incredibly boring.'

Shopping alone? Did he also live alone, then?

Just as she had when she'd first seen him on the moors, she sensed mystery in him which intrigued her against her will. Then that frisson of excitement was there again, and she tried to push it away.

For heaven's sake, what had happened to her resolve to steer clear of him? To ignore his attraction before it shattered her peace of mind? It had completely disappeared, she thought with disgust. Now here she was, actually wondering if he lived alone or if he was married and doing the shopping for some equally attractive wife.

By the look of his heavy bag she realised that he had bought enough for a large family, and felt a pain that was almost physical. Then a voice in her head told her to pull herself together. As he took her arm to steer her down the hill, despite the magnetism of his touch she clung to the fact that he was merely a colleague. And was determined that he would stay that way. She would never allow him to step into that raw space that had been left inside her when David Lawrence had gone out of her life.

After managing to miss a collision with the crowd of people who were now pushing their way towards the top of the hill, Ben drew her into a little café. Telling her that he refused to take no for an answer, he made her sit at a table by the window, and ordered scrambled eggs on toast for two with a pot of coffee.

Breathless and now really annoyed, she said, 'Why?'

'Just one word, but with a thousand expressions in it!' he remarked, unable to prevent himself from smiling at her when he should really be keeping his distance. 'By that, do I take it that I've overstepped the mark?'

'Something like that. For one thing, how do you know I wasn't planning to meet an old friend? After all, I have been to Devon before.'

'I don't know. I just hoped to get you to myself for a while. And, before you ask why again, I'll tell you it's to talk about the couple we met last night. The Browns.'

'But—coffee and scrambled eggs! How do you know I haven't already eaten?'

This time the smile was tinged with wickedness. 'I just know,' he said quietly.

'Really?'

'Yes. By the way you look, my guess is that you haven't even had breakfast. Am I right?'

'I've had coffee and biscuits,' she said defensively. 'With Dr Gilmore, as it happens.'

'Oh, right. But that won't last long, will it? So don't tell me you haven't got room for a snack lunch.'

Two steaming plates arrived, and Kate realised that she was far too hungry to refuse. So, not even waiting while Ben poured the coffee, she tackled the eggs at once.

They ate in silence for a while, then Kate asked,

'Who was that man who bumped into you?'

'The so-called vicar, you mean?' She nodded. 'He's our local eccentric. A man with many names. Some call him Crazy Colin, others Barmy Boris. He's a patient of mine so I know him as Michael Lee.'

'A gypsy name, if I ever heard one! So he really is a Romany, then?'

'That's what he believes. But he lives strictly alone. Whatever tribe he once belonged to disappeared long ago. He doesn't give much away about himself but I do know he's as educated as he sounds. When he was young he gained a degree at Exeter University but since then he's done practically nothing. Says he prefers a life with no entanglements.'

'So, what does he do for money?'

'He seems to have plenty. Where it comes from, I just don't know. Rich ancestors, maybe.'

All too soon the unexpected meal came to an end. Once she'd managed to rein in her ridiculous feelings Kate had enjoyed being with Ben. They had talked endlessly on many subjects with the kind of ease usually known only to old friends, she realised. But not once had he mentioned the Brown family.

As they left the café and walked on down the hill Kate wondered if he would talk about them now. But he didn't. He just led the way into the superstore, pointed out the layout to her and then said he'd wait by the door for her to do what she came for.

'What happened to all this "shopping alone" bit?' she said with a little laugh.

'I've had second thoughts. You'll get on better without me trailing after you.'

She shrugged as she took a trolley, wondering what on earth had happened to make him so edgy. Then she walked towards the aisles, annoyed with herself for letting his swiftly changing moods affect her like this.

Ben leant against a wall, watching her disappear. And asked himself savagely why he hadn't managed to distance himself from her. What on earth did he think he was doing?

Then, without any warning, he saw her as she'd been the first time he'd met her. Opening her car window to ask the way and looking at him with those incredible green eyes. That was the moment when he'd found breath difficult to come by.

He knew that he'd been sharp with her but he just couldn't help it. There was something about her that suddenly made him think of Janice. Not her looks, or even her mannerisms. There had been a kind of magic quality in her, and the sudden pain he'd felt had been unbearable. Then all that guilt he'd felt long ago was with him again and he wondered if he would always be haunted by memories that refused to die.

He would just have to push her from his mind, he thought savagely. Ignore the sympathy that made him want to take away the touch of sorrow he'd glimpsed in her. A woman like this deserved perfection—something he knew he could never give her. For, apart from the shame he'd managed to live with, there was still that other huge problem in his life, wasn't there? One that he knew would be with him for a long, long time.

He could see no future, except for work—and yet more work—until it dulled the senses. He would just have to rid himself of the fever that rose in him whenever she was near. It would be difficult but he knew that he must do it if he wanted any sort of inner peace.

Now he saw her coming back to the checkout with her trolley filled to the brim, that attractive smile lifting the corners of her mouth. He tried to look at her casually but felt her magnetism, pulling at him, and wondered if he would ever be free of it.

'What's all this?' he asked, trying to sound flippant as she began to unload enough food to last at least a month. 'Expecting visitors? Or a siege, perhaps?'

She laughed. 'Of course not! But you never know, do you?'

He stared at her for a moment before understanding came to him. 'Dare I guess? Is some of this for the Brown family?'

She flushed. 'Yes, actually, it is. I hope it won't embarrass them.'

He grinned, at last feeling himself relax. 'So, what do you think my shopping bag is stuffed with? I'm not expecting a siege either.'

'You mean. . .?'

'I do. The Alloway larder is always stacked up midweek. By my housekeeper.'

'Your—housekeeper?' she asked, not really meaning to pry. But her thoughts ran on. Did this mean that he had no wife, then?

She paid for her goods which Ben collected, placing them carefully into the holdall—with the eggs on top. Then she looked at him, not realising that the unspoken question was still hovering in her eyes.

As if he had read her thoughts he said gruffly, 'I have a housekeeper because I'm a widower. Most people know this, but I don't expect them to talk about it. Understood?'

'Of course,' she said, rebuffed. 'It's none of my business, is it?'

Suddenly she wished that it was. She also wished that he didn't sound so quietly angry.

As they began to toil up the hill again, with Ben carrying her bag, Kate remembered the magazine Tilly wanted, and left him on the pavement with her groceries while she whisked into a newsagent's. Looking around, she couldn't see *Magic of Our Time* anywhere so she went to the counter to ask for it. Then two things happened, both of them embarrassing.

First, the man serving her gave her a strange look, before diving beneath the counter. Then when he furtively handed over the magazine Kate saw Ben, standing at her side, now with his own shopping as well as hers.

He was watching her curiously as she paid for the magazine, so she immediately folded it lengthwise, trying—but not quite managing—to hide its title. Then she blushed as if she had been caught buying pornography.

'Well, well!' Ben murmured as they left the shop together, having insisted on carrying her bag along with his own. 'So this is the sort of thing you go in for, is it?'

'It's for Tilly Marsden,' she said hastily.

'What a shame! For a moment I thought I'd met someone with a hobby as strange as my own.'

'Writing about herbal medicine? But that's not just a hobby, is it? You're really delving into alternative medicine. Perhaps even homeopathy?'

'Maybe.' He spoke curtly, clinging to a façade of indifference. 'These days it can be quite respectable, you know. After all, the Royal London Homeopathic Hospital does actually exist. A doctor I know once studied their methods. Found them helpful, too.'

They reached her car and she watched him stow her holdall in the boot, thinking what an open mind he had. If every doctor was this honest she thought that the medical world would be a better place.

'I'm parked over there,' he said, pointing to a clump of trees. 'Shall we go separately to the Browns and give them the food we've bought for them?'

'That's fine by me! I'll meet you there, then.' She laughed softly. 'They'll think Christmas has come early!'

CHAPTER FOUR

THE last Kate saw of Ben Alloway that weekend was his car, disappearing from New Barling towards The Rowans. She had no idea where he lived, but supposed that the house he shared with the mythical housekeeper must be in the same direction.

After they had presented Maisie Brown with the groceries they'd bought and Ben had driven off she stayed on the porch for a while, trying to assure the girl that what they had done for her was no big deal.

'And you needn't pay us,' she said impulsively. 'Just think of it as a house-warming present.' She hadn't checked this with Ben, but was sure that he would agree.

'How kind you both are! I've never met doctors like you before. Where I used to live they just didn't want to know.'

'I'm sure that's not really true,' Kate said gently. 'Most doctors are terribly busy these days but that doesn't mean they don't care, you know.'

Maisie stared at her doubtfully. 'That's as maybe. But I can tell you now that I'm really looking forward to being on your list, Dr Frinton. I'll come in first thing. You see if I don't!'

On Monday, before Kate could begin work, Maurice Gilmore came to New Barling. 'Just to be sure you're properly settled in,' he said, giving her an encouraging smile which faded when he noticed that John Smith wasn't there. But, after murmuring that the missing doctor was sure to turn up soon, he added that Sheila Venables was spending the morning at The Rowans with Ben Alloway.

When he left Kate talked briefly to the receptionist and to Mary Kolinski, the practice nurse who shared sessions at both surgeries with Penny Armstrong. 'I'm expecting a Maisie Brown to register as a new patient today,' she told them both, 'so will you look out for her, please? And I need a blood sample from her. Do you have a form I can fill in?'

'Sure. There's one right here.' Mary handed her a slip of paper.

'And I'll have the registration form ready for when she arrives,' the receptionist said.

'Thanks a lot.' Smiling, Kate went to her consulting room.

Here she found a large desk with drawers filled with prescription forms and updated leaflets on various diseases. There was also a computer, identical to one she'd used in the Midlands.

She had seen this room before, soon after her interview, but hadn't really taken it all in. Now, sitting at the desk, she looked around with approval. Carpeted in a cheerful red, it had several chairs, a locked drugs cupboard, a sink with soap and towels and an examination couch which could be screened by curtains.

The whole place was light and airy, with a large window covered by a slatted blind, obscuring her from view while allowing her to see everything going on outside. Including John Smith, she noticed with amusement.

He had at last turned up and was now positively scuttling towards the surgery, looking like some furtive travelling salesman.

Switching on the computer, she heard a brief knock on her door before the receptionist came in.

'Sorry, Doctor! I'm afraid I forgot to put these ready for you,' she said, handing Kate a pile of patients' folders.

'Thanks.' Kate took them, then asked, 'You share duties with someone at The Rowans, don't you?'

'Yes. I'm one of two. We also man the phones.'

'So, are you June Cranworth or the other one? I met so many people after my interview that I haven't really sorted them all out yet.'

'Not to worry! Yes, I'm June Cranworth—the newest one here. Betty Green is at The Rowans this morning. But there's no chance you'll mistake her for me because she's gorgeous! Long blonde hair, blue eyes—the lot!'

'You're not so bad yourself! What's wrong with a short brown bob and hazel eyes? To say nothing of legs going all the way to your armpits!'

June laughed. 'You've a great sense of humour, Doctor! I can see we're going to get along just fine.'

She left on another chuckle of laughter, and Kate glanced hastily through the folders. Then, using an intercom connected to the waiting room, she called in her first patient.

This was Liz Burrows, a young married woman, who seemed tense with nerves. She was also uncommunicative, and after a few moments Kate despaired of ever getting her to speak.

'So, please tell me what I can do for you, Mrs Burrows,' she said when most of her previous questions had gone unanswered. 'I'm afraid I really can't help if you don't talk to me.'

The woman's face suddenly flushed with anger, and she snapped aggressively, 'You're all the same, aren't you? Acting like God Almighty! What do you know about us ordinary folk?'

Puzzled, Kate asked quietly, 'Are you thinking of someone in particular, Mrs Burrows?'

'No. It's all the doctors here. Know-alls, the lot of you! I thought, being new here, you'd at least be different.'

Kate looked again at the woman's notes, saw that she had already been seen by Sheila Venables and John Smith and that psychiatric treatment had been suggested. But this hadn't been followed up.

'I see that you're registered with Dr Smith. Yet the secretary sent your notes to me. Did you ask for me specially?'

The woman shrugged. 'Thought I'd give you a try. It's not against the law, is it? You're a team, aren't you?'

'Of course. And I'll be pleased to help you. But, as I said, there's not much I can do unless you let me know how you're feeling, is there?'

After staring at her with a strange unblinking defiance the woman became sullen and withdrawn, pulling at her fingers and then locking them together before forcing them into her lap. A moment later she held her head high, and Kate noticed a slight swelling in her neck. Then she looked through the slatted blind, just staring at nothing.

Kate had met this sort of behaviour before, usually with teenagers disturbed by rapid changes in their bodies which also affected their emotional stability. The few fully grown adults she had seen with similar symptoms had been suffering from very definite mental sickness.

But somehow she felt instinctively that the root cause of Mrs Burrows's trouble was not in her mind but in her body. Nevertheless, she wanted to get a whole picture—to find out if all this aggression and the pallor which had suddenly replaced her angry flush were signs of organic disease or perhaps due to some real tragedy in her life.

'Have you suffered any emotional upset recently?' she asked quietly.

'And if I have? What's that got to do with anything?'

'Maybe nothing. But, on the other hand, it could be causing you to be uptight like this.'

The woman suddenly stood up. 'I'm not uptight!' she shouted, leaning over the desk and glaring at Kate with bulging grey eyes which looked as if they had turned to stone. 'I'm just angry with the whole lot of you. Stuffing me with pills that don't do any good. Smiling, like you are now, when all the time you really. . .despise me!'

She looked as if she was about to lash out so Kate moved her hand nearer to an emergency button hidden beneath the desk.

But at that moment the unexpected happened. Sitting down again as her eyes filled with tears, the woman suddenly crumpled. Throwing her arms on the desk, she hid her face and began to sob. Every now and then her body shuddered as she drew in a noisy breath.

Grabbing some tissues, Kate went round the desk and knelt beside her, took her in her arms and dabbed at her wet eyes. 'There, there!' she murmured softly, as if she were trying to comfort a child. 'Just stay here for a few moments, and I'll see if I can rustle up a cup of tea.'

But before she could move there was a knock on her door, followed by Mary Kolinski's swift entrance. Looking anxious, the practice nurse said, 'I heard a noise, Doctor. Is anything wrong?'

'Not really, but thanks for coming. Is there a place where my patient can sit quietly before I see her again? Over a cup of tea, preferably.'

'Of course. My own room's empty so she can stay with me. And don't worry, Dr Frinton. I'll look after her, then call you when she's ready to come back.'

The nurse coaxed Mrs Burrows away from the desk and Kate saw her relax a little. She'll be all right, she thought with relief as she heard Mary say softly, 'It's Liz Burrows, isn't it? I met you once in the community centre. That party last Christmas, remember?'

When they'd left Kate went through Mrs Burrows's notes again, concentrating on everything that had been prescribed for her. She seemed to have received treatment for a number of conditions, from flu-like symptoms which came to nothing to persistent colds and various aches and pains which led nowhere. She had also been given a variety of tablets and capsules, including anti-depressants. The final suggestion had been to 'get a good tonic from the chemist'.

Kate noticed that this entry had been made by John Smith, and wondered how he dared to record such a vague suggestion. Surely this sort of treatment had gone out with the Ark! Had John found the patient so impossible that he'd decided to pass her on and hope for the best?

Whatever the reason, it just wasn't good enough. The woman was either a malingerer or she wasn't. If she wasn't then something very real and nasty could be happening to her. Maybe at the next practice meeting she could discuss this case with Maurice Gilmore, Kate thought, determined to get to the bottom of the problem.

She left her room to find Mary Kolinski and see how her patient was doing.

But Mrs Burrows had fled.

'I tried to hang onto her but she just wouldn't stay put, I'm afraid,' Mary said. 'She seems to have a real hatred of medics, doesn't she?'

'Tell me about it! I gather from her notes that she's seen quite a few of us without success. Why she came here today beats me.'

'It's simple, Doctor,' Mary said, giving a wry smile. 'She saw her chance to harangue someone new, I'd say.'

'Well, at least she got a cup of tea out of us!'

'And that's another thing. After telling me that she never drinks milk, she calmly emptied the tea down my sink then flounced out.'

A bid for attention? Or something much more serious? Kate just didn't know, and was more than a little annoyed with herself. Her first patient of the day—with no result whatsoever! Perhaps Maisie Brown would be more rewarding.

But even that proved negative. When Kate went to Reception she found that the girl hadn't arrived 'first thing', as she promised. Neither June nor Mary had seen her.

'That's a pity!' Kate said. 'I wanted to take her blood early on, then send it to be analysed pronto!'

'How urgent is it?' Mary asked.

'Fairly. But I guess it can wait till tomorrow. I'll call

on her this afternoon and have a chat. Shall I take the registration form at the same time?' she suggested to June Cranworth. 'Or are you a stickler for secretarial staff doing it?'

'Not at all.' June handed Kate the appropriate paper then asked, 'Shall I send in your next patient?'

'Please! But just give me a moment to catch my breath.'

And so the morning went on, with Kate listening to wheezy chests and advising mothers of young children about cough syrup which was easily obtainable from the chemist's. She expected to see the common cold in early spring like this, but not in such numbers. By the time she had examined at least six children with nothing more dire than runny noses she began to wonder if this was their way of avoiding school.

But as she examined yet another young boy and heard him give a harsh, dry cough she changed her mind.

Sitting beside his mother—a quiet, well-spoken woman whose notes were also included so Kate supposed that this was a double appointment—five-year-old Charlie Webb was flushed and uncomfortable. His pulse was abnormally rapid so Kate slipped a thermometer under his tongue, which was coated and looking far from healthy.

His open mouth also revealed Koplik's spots which were just beginning to develop against the inside of his cheeks, giving the appearance of small white flecks. She looked closely at the boy's eyes, which seemed sore and were slightly red, then lifted his T-shirt. Here she saw the beginnings of a rash.

'I thought as much,' Kate murmured to herself. Then,

to Mrs Webb, she said, 'My advice to you is to go straight home and put this young man to bed. Keep him warm, shut out any bright sunlight to protect his eyes, give him plenty to drink and let him sleep for as long as he likes.'

She removed the thermometer, saw the lad's raised temperature and added, 'He also needs an antipyretic to control his fever so I suggest you give him small doses of children's aspirin.'

'But—what's wrong with him, Doctor?'

'I'm afraid he's developing measles, Mrs Webb.'

For a moment the woman looked stunned. Then she said, '*Measles*? But he had jabs for that when he was younger! Are you sure, Doctor? It's the last thing I would've expected.'

'I think you'll find I'm right,' Kate said patiently. 'But if you'd like another opinion I can ask Dr Smith to take a look at him.'

'Oh, no, I trust you, Doctor. It just seems so strange when he's been immunised.'

Kate went to the sink, shook down the thermometer, ran cold water over it and then dipped it in a jar of disinfectant, before replacing it in its case. Afterwards, washing her hands, she tried to think of ways to allay Mrs Webb's fears.

At last she said, 'Immunisation isn't a complete guarantee against the disease, I'm afraid. The virus gets used to the vaccine, you know, and fights against it. But because your Charlie had his inoculation early on this attack may be very slight. But, even so, it means that he mustn't mix with other children until he's better. Especially young babies.' Then she added as an afterthought, 'Have you other children in the house?'

'No, Doctor. There's only Charlie. Not because we didn't try, mind you. We did, but it came to nothing. Now it's too late because I'm past all that.'

Kate couldn't believe this. The information on Mrs Webb's documents listed her as a woman in her middle thirties. 'It's not really too late, you know,' she said quietly. 'So, if you need advice, why not pop into our Well Woman Clinic one Wednesday?'

Mrs Webb gave Kate a sad smile. 'You probably haven't had time to read all my notes yet, have you, Doctor?' Kate shook her head briefly. 'Well, then, you won't know that I've had a hysterectomy.'

'I see. Why was that?'

'Heavy bleeding. Month after month. I found it quite exhausting, Doctor.'

'I'm sure you did, Mrs Webb,' Kate said sympathetically. Then she went through the notes swiftly, found what she was looking for and said, 'I see Dr Venables dealt with you at that time. And that your operation was in Plymouth. I expect you were told why it was necessary?'

'Oh, yes. The doctors there said I had fibroids.'

'And did they tell you what they were?'

'Well, not exactly. Just said they were growths in the womb. Does this mean they—could have spread to some other part of my body?'

The woman began to look so scared that Kate said quickly, 'I don't think so, Mrs Webb. They're usually benign.'

'But they took the whole womb away. And I thought. . .'

Kate smiled, trying to reassure her. 'Surgeons sometimes have to do a hysterectomy when there are so many fibroids that they're difficult to remove. But this doesn't mean the growths are necessarily cancerous.'

'I see. So. . .is everything all right now?'

Kate glanced at a hospital report. 'It seems so. And I see you had a post-operational check at the hospital.' Mrs Webb nodded. 'Didn't the consultant tell you that everything was OK? Then give you time to ask questions?'

'Not really. I found it difficult to talk to him.'

Even now she looked as if she couldn't believe she was in the clear so Kate decided to discuss the hospital notes more fully with her. As Charlie was now getting restless she found a box of children's toys, which every consulting room seemed to possess, and took out a thick wooden jigsaw puzzle to occupy him. When he was squatting on the floor, thoroughly engrossed, she turned back to Mrs Webb.

'You're worried, aren't you?' she murmured.

'Yes. It's silly of me, I know. But, you see, I found everything so difficult that I never got round to asking the right questions. Jack, my husband, told me I should have done but I was too confused when I was there. And, anyway, everyone seemed so busy that I just didn't want to bother them.'

Poor woman, Kate thought. As scared as hell when there was really no need. She turned back to the hospital file, read through it more carefully this time then said, 'According to this, everything is perfectly clear. It's written down here in black and white so you've really no need to worry.'

Kate had no doubt that the surgeon had reassured Mrs

Webb at some point. But he may not have realised that she was too upset to listen properly. He would also have expected the woman's GP to talk it through with her. Quite obviously this hadn't happened for Mrs Webb had not been to the surgery recently. Quite a dangerous loophole, Kate thought, and one which should definitely be discussed at a meeting.

Kate studied Mrs Webb for a moment. The fear had now gone out of her eyes but she looked tired and depressed. 'How are you eating?' she asked.

'Quite well, Doctor, though I don't really enjoy my food. By the time I've tackled the housework and the washing I'm too tired to enjoy anything.'

'I see.' Kate imagined a gleaming house with nothing out of place, food ready for her husband the moment he returned from work but precious little energy left to eat her own meal. 'What if you let the house look after itself for a while? Went for a walk sometimes instead of working so hard? Would that be so terrible?'

The woman gave a wan smile. 'That's what Jack's always telling me. Says there are more important things in life. But I don't know... Although we live on the New Barling estate we bought our house, you see. And I want to look after it properly.' She paused, giving a small sigh. 'Anyway, my mother brought me up to do these things well. Told me no man wants a slut.'

Kate laughed softly. 'I'm sure no one could accuse you of being that, Mrs Webb. May I suggest that your husband might be pleased if you eased off a little? No man wants a slave for a wife, you know.'

'Are you married, Doctor?'

Taken aback, Kate admitted that she wasn't. And

immediately saw a vivid mental picture of David Lawrence. The might-have-been who could still fill her with yearning. She wondered why she had seen that image now, then realised that the word 'slave' had triggered it.

Not for the first time she told herself that, despite all the emptiness inside her, she had really had a lucky escape. For, after months of living with the man, she too had been in danger of becoming his slave. And had gradually realised that, despite all his heated denials, this was exactly what he'd wanted.

At last she came out of her dream and concentrated on Mrs Webb. 'I'll visit Charlie before the end of the week, just to see how he's doing,' she said. 'But if you're not happy about him please ring and I'll come straight over. Meanwhile, I think you need a course of vitamins. They'll help your general condition, and hopefully bring back your appetite.'

When Kate's long list of patients came to an end it was well after midday. But before she could go back to her flat for something to eat there were things to do, such as checking notes on the computer and then duplicating them in the folders for cross-reference. When this was done she still had to go to Reception to see if any of the patients Maurice had allocated to her had rung through, asking for visits.

'There's just one today, Doctor. A man with a damaged foot,' June Cranworth said. 'Lives some way outside the village and has no phone. So a neighbour rang through for him—a woman who apparently found him in a ditch and helped him back home.'

'And didn't send for an ambulance?'

'She said the man wouldn't have it. Told her to ring here and ask for you.'

'Me? In person?'

June laughed softly. 'Seems you made a hit with him. Though how he comes to know you the caller wouldn't say.'

Baffled, Kate stared at her. 'So, who is this fan?'

Handing Kate a slip of paper, June said, 'Michael Lee.'

'But he's Dr Alloway's patient! I met him on Saturday while we were shopping in Tanwyth.'

'You were *shopping* with Ben Alloway?' June began to look amused.

'No, of course not,' Kate said quickly. 'We just met up by chance.'

June was now grinning openly at her, unsettling Kate so that she blushed with embarrassment. 'Wonders will never cease,' the girl said succinctly. 'No one—and I do mean *no one*—ever gets to spend time with our glamorous doctor, even by accident. Not many people have had the slightest glimpse of his home either. But there you are—that's our mysterious Dr Alloway for you!'

An outside door opened on a gust of springtime wind and a deep voice asked, 'Who's taking my name in vain?'

Kate spun round to find herself facing Ben and suddenly felt like a child, caught with her fingers in the jam pot.

'Oh, nothing sinister, I promise you,' she said hastily. 'It seems that one of your patients has asked for me. But I'm sure it's a mistake that can be ironed out in no time.'

'Who is it?'

'Michael Lee. The so-called priest of Tanwyth I met at the weekend.'

'That old devil! Why does he want a visit?'

'Apparently he fell into a ditch and hurt his ankle, Doctor,' June said.

'Is it urgent?'

'I don't think so. A woman friend rang for him and said she'd made him comfortable. Then she very definitely asked for Dr Frinton. At least, I suppose that's who she meant, though she didn't actually say the name. Just asked for the new lady doctor.'

Ben turned to Kate, a wicked smile lighting up his deep blue eyes. 'Must have taken a shine to you! I always did suspect him of being a ladies' man!'

'And you don't mind? That he didn't ask for you, I mean.'

'Not at all. I'm perfectly happy to share one of Devon's zaniest characters. But do you think you could find your way to his van? It's so well hidden that I spent hours looking for it the first time I went there.'

'In that case, perhaps you could give me directions.'

'Better still, what if I come with you? Oh, I won't interfere, of course. I don't harbour chauvinistic thoughts about women doctors, I swear.'

Kate looked at him, wondering if that was really true. Even in these enlightened days some male doctors still secretly mistrusted women in their profession. Take her brothers, for instance. They'd never believed that she would really become a GP.

But Ben's eyes were clear, his face devoid of any deceit whatsoever.

'That sounds a good idea,' she said at last. 'Shall we use your car or mine?'

'Mine, I think. Then I can introduce you to an even

better idea. As the case isn't urgent we'll have lunch on the way.'

Kate didn't know what this would entail, but liked the sound of it. A few moments later, managing to ignore the cheeky smile on June's face, she found herself being driven through some extremely narrow lanes to the Farmer's Castle—an attractive pub a few miles away.

CHAPTER FIVE

BEN parked the car in a layby and they walked the short distance to the Farmer's Castle. Kate thought the wonderful thing about it was that it really did look like a castle. Not far from Little Medington, it was square and solid—built of stone with ornamental turrets running round the edges of a flat roof. And its facia was just as imposing. With narrow windows of uneven glass and a huge oak door, sporting a heavy iron handle, it looked like something from the past. Which it really was, Kate realised as she read a date carved into one wall.

'It's absolutely perfect! So unspoilt,' she said, her eyes shining. 'But what's significant about that date? Was 1814 the year this place was built?

'Heavens, no! It was here long before then. That date was put there to remind everyone of the year Napoleon was banished to Elba.'

'*Napoleon*? But why him?'

Ben led her through the door to a low-ceilinged room with ancient oak beams and comfortable furniture covered in red plush. 'That famous gentleman made quite an impact on Devon, you know,' he said, smiling. 'The prison at Princetown, which we all call "Dartmoor", was originally built to hold French soldiers captured by us in the Napoleonic Wars.'

Kate was silent, feeling horribly ignorant. Then she asked, 'So what happened to the men after the wars?'

'They probably went home—though there is a legend about some of them, staying here and marrying Devon women.' He shrugged. 'Anyway, it's all in the distant past. Too learned for me, so I think I'll stick to modern medicine.'

After he'd been to the bar to order two plates of crusty bread with cheese, salad and pickle, he brought the lemonade Kate had asked for and a small glass of beer for himself, setting them on an oak table. As they sat near a huge open hearth with a roaring log fire Kate felt herself relaxing.

'I'm pleased to find someone as ignorant as I am about history,' she said, warmed not only by the fire but also by a special sort of camaraderie growing between them. 'I usually have to put up with not very polite remarks when people see my limitations.'

He grinned. 'I can't really believe that. Who on earth would dare to challenge you?'

'Oh, quite a few! Including my three brainy brothers! They're all doctors, and just can't get used to the idea of their little sister also making the grade. They're all specialists now. So how's that for one-upmanship?'

'I can only say thank God I don't have that sort of ambition. Nothing on earth would make me give up general practice. Though at one time my wife did try to tempt me. But I resisted.'

'She was a doctor?'

'No. A nursing sister,' he said briefly, then picked up his drink, studying it as if he had found something interesting floating there and couldn't move his eyes away.

It seemed that the mere mention of his late wife caused

him to frown, and Kate watched as a dark shadow passed over his eyes. She wondered what sort of woman his wife had been, then pushed the thought away impatiently. Whatever influence she still had over Ben was nothing to do with her.

But you wish it was, don't you? Go on, admit it! The voice in her head was loud and insistent. Mocking her. Telling her to ignore her vow never to trust in a man again.

Now she realised that Ben had been speaking to her and she hadn't heard a word. 'I'm sorry,' she apologised. 'You were saying. . .?'

He looked solemn. 'I'm the one who should be apologising. For intruding on a dream you seemed to be having. About your brothers, was it?'

'Er—yes,' she lied. 'My parents, too. They were both so adventurous that I find it hard to live up to them.'

'Sounds intriguing. I take it they're also in medicine?'

'They were. But they died some time ago.'

It was strange but somehow she no longer found it difficult to speak of them. The trauma of their violent deaths seemed to have lost its hold over her, and she found herself talking quite openly to Ben.

'My mother was an obstetrician who spent her early professional years in South America, where my father was researching leishmaniasis,' she said. 'They married, then came back here when she was pregnant. After that my father wrote books on his pet subject, and lectured about it in medical schools all over the world. When we were all grown up Mum sometimes went with him.'

Ben gazed at her in disbelief. Then he said, 'You mean your father was the famous Scott Frinton?'

She gave an embarrassed little laugh. 'Yes, I suppose he was well known. But as kids we were very irreverent and used to call him "Sandy Scott". Because of his research into leishmaniasis, of course.'

'I'm afraid I'm not well up in tropical medicine. But I do know the disease is transmitted by the bite of the South American sandfly. Hence the nickname, I suppose?' She nodded briefly. 'I must say I admire doctors who spend their lives doing research like this. But it's never been my cup of tea.'

'Nor mine.'

'But one day you'd like to specialise in some other branch of medicine like your brothers?'

'I used to think so. But not any more. Though I did spend some time at a children's hospital, which I enjoyed immensely. Was even tempted to go in for paediatrics. But once having been bitten by the bug of general practice I decided that was what I really wanted. I just love the variety, you see.'

'You also love people, don't you?'

'Yes,' she said quietly, and watched a kind of deep sadness come into his eyes.

She thought it was there because of his dead wife, and wanted to stretch out a hand to him. To tell him that she had felt the same kind of devastation when her parents had died in the air crash that had robbed her of their love. She had no idea how Ben's wife had died, but she wanted to say that people eventually got through their mourning—even though a touch of sadness always remained deep inside.

She almost spoke but stopped herself when she saw him frowning. Then the barman brought over their snacks, and she turned her attention to the food as if this were the most important thing in her life.

'So, how did your first surgery go?' he asked, and she saw the tension leave him. She then launched into a series of vivid descriptions of various patients. This at last brought a smile to his face and then a look of horror when she told him of her fear of being attacked by an angry Mrs Burrows.

'Oh, don't look so worried,' Kate said with a grin. 'She was the one to cry her eyes out in the end. Though I must admit her condition worries me. So much so that I'd like to discuss her case at a practice meeting. And, while we're on the subject of patients, I thought I'd call on Maisie Brown this afternoon. She didn't come in to register today, and I find that quite worrying too.'

'Like me to come with you when we've been to see Michael Lee?'

'You'd really do that? But won't it be taking up too much of your time?'

'Not at all. I've cleared my afternoon specially for you. Maurice Gilmore thought it would be a good idea.'

'Because I'm new and don't know my way around yet? Or does he want you to keep an eye on me?' Her voice grew sharp as she remembered John Smith's fixation with the Gestapo. Then she pushed the thought away, telling herself not to be so stupid.

'You make me sound like a gaoler, woman!' Ben said with a grin. 'When all I want to be is a helpful colleague.'

'Sorry. I really must try not to be so suspicious!'

'So colleague it is, then?' he asked, stretching out his hand.

'Yes. Colleague it is.' She put her hand in his and he

shook it. But she wished he hadn't. The touch of his skin on hers was too electric for her peace of mind. Then he suddenly snatched his own hand away and she saw that darkness in him again.

When they had finished their lunch in silence he gave her a look which was purely professional and said seriously, 'Maybe we should skip coffee and get down to business.'

'Of course,' she agreed. She was awed by the authority she heard in his voice—even more than by the swift changes of mood she kept witnessing.

Why was he like this? All sweetness and light one moment, then looking at her as if he couldn't bear to be near her the next. She was tempted to snap at him, telling him that she too could be temperamental. But she stopped herself. Such childish behaviour wasn't really part of her nature and she was damned if she would make a fool of herself now.

Trying to keep a tight rein on her feelings, she rose from the table, thanked him for the food and followed him to the car.

'Barmy Boris', as Kate still privately thought of him, had set up home in the most dilapidated caravan she'd ever come across. It was perched on the far edge of a field, and as they peered over the top of a gate she realised how solitary it was. With no sign of any neighbours, she thought that if he hadn't been found in a ditch by the elusive woman who had phoned the surgery he could well have been in real danger for a long time.

'What makes a man want to live in an isolated place

like this?' she asked as they walked over rough grass, trying to avoid potholes.

'Because he's self-sufficient, perhaps?'

'That's all very well. I like to live alone, but I make sure there's someone else within calling distance.'

'You've never married?' he asked suddenly. Then he apologised for being so intrusive and turned away from her, his eyes shadowed.

He was respecting her need for privacy, wasn't he? She could understand that, and recognised a similar need in him. Answering questions about one's private life like this could bring very real pain. But strangely she felt that she would welcome them from him, and this surprised her.

Yet the idea also struck a warning note somewhere deep inside her. Did she really want to become so intimate with another human being? Give anyone even a glimpse of the darkness still lying deep inside her?

At last she found that she couldn't deal with the shame she saw in him because he'd broached such a personal subject so she said, 'It's a perfectly natural thing to ask.' Then, gathering up her courage, she managed to add, 'And the answer is no, I've never been married. I was once engaged to a fellow medic. But—it just didn't work out.'

'I'm sorry.'

'Don't be. In the end I was relieved. It was all a terrible mistake.'

They left it there, and although he looked as if he wanted to ask more she was glad when he didn't.

They reached the caravan and Ben rapped on the door, before opening it to reveal a scene of pristine cleanliness where Kate had expected to find squalor. Michael Lee was lying on a folding bed, his fancy-dress clothes hanging on a peg in one corner. Now wearing jeans and T-shirt, partly concealed by a tartan rug spread over him, he sat up and stared at Ben with a look of sheer disappointment.

'I told old Maud to ask for the new lady doctor. Not you!' he said accusingly.

'Don't worry,' Ben said, laughter in his voice, 'Dr Frinton's here too, you old devil!'

'Oh, good! Just the sight of her will make me better, I'm quite sure.'

'Strictly speaking, you're Dr Alloway's patient,' Kate said, resting her medical bag on a stool by the bed.

'Then I'd like to be transferred immediately!'

Ben looked straight at him. Kate saw him trying hard to smother his laughter, and wasn't surprised when a sort of quiet hiccup escaped from him. But at last he managed to look solemn as he said, 'I'm afraid that would be difficult and time-wasting. It entails quite a lot of paperwork and a great deal of tedious officialdom.'

'What a load of codswallop!' Michael Lee exclaimed.

The coarse words, spoken in his highly educated accent, sounded utterly incongruous. As Ben stared at him he flushed, then turned to Kate and apologised.

'What for?' she asked, baffled.

'For my bad language, my dear. I don't usually talk like this in front of a lady.'

Kate grinned at him. 'I've heard far worse in my time, Mr Lee.'

The man grunted. 'You surprise me. But I really must protest. I find all this form-filling quite unnecessary.

So what do you propose to do about it?'

'Nothing at the moment. Not until I tell Dr Gilmore, our senior partner. And certainly not unless Dr Alloway agrees.'

The part-gypsy, part-vicar and part-hundreds of other things suddenly stared at her with a solemn expression. Then he said with a touch of reverence, 'I admire your loyalty, my girl!'

'Thank you. But what about yours? Just tell me why you'd prefer me as your doctor. There's absolutely nothing wrong with my partner here.'

Michael Lee chuckled. 'Oh, but there is, my dear! For a start, he doesn't wear skirts.'

Suddenly speechless, Kate was glad when Ben took over, telling the man not to be such an old fool and motioning to Kate to begin her examination.

'You're sure about this?' she murmured to him quietly.

'If that's what the wretched man wants then he shall have it!' Ben was now speaking so loudly that Michael couldn't possibly miss what he was saying. 'And don't pull any punches, Dr Frinton. It's time he learnt that women doctors can be as exacting as men. Then perhaps he'll decide to stop play-acting like this.'

He sounded severe but Kate saw a touch of humour in him and went along with his game for a while. She was gentle when necessary but certainly didn't let that stop her giving the man a very thorough and full examination. After she had listened to his chest, taken his pulse and flipped down a lower eyelid to find good healthy colour she turned her attention to the ankle that was supposedly damaged.

It was then she realised that Michael Lee had come

near to making a fool of her and was glad that Ben was there.

'There's absolutely nothing wrong with your foot, Mr Lee,' she said severely. 'I think you've been wasting our time. If we were the police we could consider prosecuting you for this kind of offence. Being a doctor, I can't. But I'd better warn you that it is my duty to write all this up in your notes. And, of course, I will most certainly bring it up with our senior partner.'

She had the satisfaction of seeing the man wilt. A moment later she asked herself just why he had engineered all this rigmarole. Was he seeking company because he was lonely? Or was there some psychological problem she hadn't spotted?

Looking seriously at Ben, she said, 'May we have a few words in private?'

'Of course.' He told the man that they needed to consult, suggested that he lie there patiently and whisked Kate outside. He could scarcely contain his laughter as he said, 'So you've sussed the old devil out! And not before time, I'd say.'

'But, Ben, I'm just not sure. He might have pulled this trick for some very good reason. Have you spotted anything that may be very badly wrong with him?'

'Oh, yes. He's lovesick! His libido is working overtime.'

'No—seriously, I mean.'

'I am being serious. He's lonely, he's seen an attractive woman for the first time in ages and he's making a play for you. I'm sure that's all it is.'

'But is he entirely—balanced? You say he's highly educated, yet he lives like—this!'

'It's what he wants, Kate. The choice is his. As for being unbalanced. . .well, I think he's merely eccentric.' Ben studied her for a moment, then said, 'I think you'll just have to get used to the fact that many people in this area don't exactly meet the norm. It's a place filled with nonconformists, you know, ranging from artists and writers to New-Age travellers. All of them imaginative.'

'And none of this bothers you?'

'Not really. I worked in London for some time, often meeting people you just couldn't measure with a conventional yardstick. Coming here was different, of course. But people are people wherever one goes. Dear old "Barmy Boris" has many a counterpart in London, you know.'

'So—what about me taking him on as a patient? Would you approve of that?'

'Er—not entirely. Oh, not that I think you wouldn't be able to cope with him, of course. But—well, you could find him something of a handful. And, believe me, he can be tedious, too.

'So, how about keeping him on your list and sharing him with me if he insists?'

'Great! He mostly turns up at The Rowans, but there's nothing to stop him making an appointment at New Barling. After all, they are twin surgeries.'

'Oh, right. So the problem's solved.'

'Until he decides to make a real bid for you! The moment that happens promise to let me know. Then I'll do my best to rescue you!'

She laughed at a vision she saw of Ben in shining armour. 'I can just see you riding a stallion,' she spluttered. 'I only hope it has more staying power than the horse Mr Lee told me about. She died, he said, and that's why he stays put like this.' She paused as another thought came to her and asked, 'By the way, how does he get to the surgery?'

'He walks,' Ben said. 'Now, shall we go back in and tell the old devil what we've arranged?'

By the time they had sorted out 'Barmy Boris' and his problems it was getting late, and Kate worried that her visit to Maisie Brown might delay her early evening surgery.

'Could we find a phone box on our way?' she asked as they got into the car again. 'I'd like to call in to warn Reception I might be delayed.'

'Hasn't Maurice issued you with a mobile phone yet?' Ben asked.

'No. I didn't realise I was entitled to one. In my last job we were expected to use our own but I never got round to it.'

'Well, here we get one as a matter of course. I'll chase it up for you, if you like.'

'Thanks! I'd be grateful if you would.'

'No problem. Meanwhile, you can use mine if we get terribly delayed.'

They arrived at the Browns' house and Kate rang the bell twice but got no answer. Just as she was about to turn away the front door opened a crack and a pale face, filled with weariness, peered at her.

'Dr Frinton!' Maisie said, her eyes filling with a kind of fear and her voice sounding husky. 'And Dr Alloway, too! I didn't hear you ring. Just saw a shadow outside the window. I'm so sorry. I must have dropped off or something.'

'Not to worry!' Kate said. 'We just wondered how you were feeling. Did you find it too difficult to come to the surgery this morning?'

Maisie's pale face flushed, then lost its colour almost immediately. 'I'm so sorry! I didn't forget. But when Joe's mate called for him as usual I really didn't feel well enough to come out.'

'Shall we go inside?' Kate suggested.

'Oh, of course! I should have asked you in before. So sorry!'

Kate slid past the pitifully thin body and stepped into the hall, with Ben following. 'Shall I make you some tea?' she suggested.

'Er—no, thanks. I had some this morning,' the girl said, 'but it made me sick.'

Ben raised his eyebrows at Kate, then asked, 'Does this often happen, Mrs Brown?'

'Only recently, Doctor. It seems to come after I feel faint. Like I did in the pub.'

'And now?'

Maisie gave them both a thin, pathetic smile. 'Yes, I do feel a bit swimmy. D'you mind if I sit down?'

'We'd be only too pleased if you did,' Ben said, taking the girl's arm to lead her into the living room and then settling her gently into a chair. 'There, now! Does that feel better?'

Maisie nodded, sinking against a cushion. Then she apologised again for 'messing them about' that morning. 'But when I got up I found I could hardly stand,' she said, 'so I wouldn't have lasted two minutes in the surgery.'

Kate looked around the room, spotted a phone and said quietly, 'You should have rung us, Maisie. Someone would have come immediately.'

'I really didn't want to bother anybody.'

'My dear girl,' Ben murmured, 'you must just get it into your head that doctors are here to help you.'

'Even though it's hard to say what I'm feeling?'

'Especially then. It's a doctor's job to find out everything about you. And to care for you in all sorts of ways. Not just treat the things that everybody can see but all those other things too.'

The girl had begun to look scared so Kate chipped in with, 'That's not to say that there's anything *mysterious* about illness. In your case the thing that's making you so tired is probably something quite simple.'

'Do—you know what it might be, Doctor?'

'Well, you may be lacking iron—which isn't always too serious. In your case I think it may be because you're pregnant. Am I right?'

Maisie looked stunned for a moment. Then she gave a trembling smile. 'A baby? A real live baby? How wonderful!' she exclaimed, her eyes beginning to shine with excitement.

'You had no idea?' Kate asked quietly.

'Not really. I've never been what you might call regular. Joe and I had hoped, of course.' A dreamy look came into the girl's eyes, and Kate marvelled at the innocence of her. She looked like a picture of a saint, Kate thought. Pure and untried, with a wonderful kind of patience that shone in eyes which were no longer lacking lustre.

'So your husband will be pleased, then?'

'He'll be over the moon, Dr Frinton!'

'Well, the sooner you sign up with a doctor the better it will be.'

'Then I'll come tomorrow. I promise!'

'There's no need for that. Look, I've brought the registration form with me.' Kate took it from her case and handed it over. 'I would also like you to have a blood test. One of the practice nurses can do this first thing tomorrow. It'll only take a moment or two.'

'But—what will she do? Will it hurt?' Maisie's voice was husky again.

'She'll just make a little scratch and draw off a small amount of blood, that's all. It won't hurt any more than if you pricked your finger with a sewing needle. And I'll make sure she knows to get you a hot drink afterwards. So there'll be no fear of you fainting again.'

Maisie looked at her with solemn eyes. Then her face suddenly shone with the most beautiful smile Kate thought she had ever witnessed. It was like the simple pleasure she'd only ever seen on a baby's face. Utterly trusting. Full of uncomplicated loving. And it moved Kate so much that for a moment she had to look away from this child-woman.

On their way to Ben's car Kate was silent, not noticing his concern until he said, 'Please don't take this the wrong way, Katie, but I'm really worried about you.'

Not many people called her Katie—as her father had always done. It shook her. Yet, in some strange way, it also pleased her.

'Worried? But why?' she asked.

'Because of the way you take your patients' troubles so much to heart. I know it's very commendable but

I'd hate to see you getting hurt by them. By anyone, come to that.'

She stayed silent on the way back to the surgery. Thinking of his words. Not really believing in the care she'd heard in his voice. Then she wondered if what he'd said was really some kind of reproval.

When he eventually dropped her off he left the car to open the passenger door and waited courteously as she got out. She saw him staring at her, his eyes kindling with a kind of dull fire. As if he didn't like what he saw. Then his expression grew blank, and she thought that he wasn't really seeing her at all.

Slowly he went back to the driver's seat. Then, waving briefly, he sped towards The Rowans without uttering another word.

And she just stood there, looking after him. Puzzled by what he had said. And feeling rejected because of the cavalier way he had left.

CHAPTER SIX

WHEN her last patient left that night Kate looked around for Mary Kolinski, but found that she had already gone.

'Is there a number I can ring?' she asked June Cranworth, who was still in Reception.

'Sure. She should be home by now.' June handed her a slip of paper.

'And she won't mind me phoning at this time of night?'

June chuckled. 'Of course not. She's not some kind of dragon, you know!'

Smiling to herself, Kate rang from her surgery, apologised for interrupting the nurse's free time and asked if she could call on Maisie Brown first thing tomorrow. 'I really do need that blood sample before I start her treatment for anaemia,' she said.

'Sure I can!' Mary said cheerfully. 'And, please, never worry about calling me at home. I'm always ready to help.'

'Thanks! I promise not to overwork you. I'll write up the tests I want and leave the form in Reception for you. Could you attach it to the sample for me then send it off?'

'Of course. Hang on a minute while I get my diary. Then I can let you know which path lab we'll be using. We take it in turns with other surgeries to prevent congestion.'

As Kate waited she thought what a pleasant soul Mary

was, and wondered vaguely how she came to have a name that sounded Polish.

'Got it!' Mary said at last. 'As it's Tuesday tomorrow it'll be Plymouth. I'll send it off by courier the moment I get it.'

'Thanks a lot,' Kate said. 'I owe you, so how about a coffee together some time?'

'Great! I'll catch you later. Perhaps next week? Then you can tell me all about yourself.'

Kate stiffened. 'There's not much to tell,' she said warily. 'But you—well, that's a different matter. I'd really love to know how you got that fascinating surname.'

'Simple! It was my Polish grandfather's. He was a great guy. I'll tell you all about him one day, if you like. That is, if you can stand the blood and guts that went with that name! Not now, though. It would take all night and I owe myself some sleep!'

Blood and guts? As she rang off Kate wondered what Mary meant. Tempted to have an early night herself, she left her evening notes in Reception, along with Maisie Brown's completed registration form and information about the blood sample. Back in her flat she rustled up a snack supper of eggs and pasta, then fell into bed, exhausted. But sleep eluded her. And all because of Ben's words as he'd brought her back from the Browns' house.

Tossing on a mattress that had once been comfortable, but now felt as if it had been made from barbed wire, she went through a whole gamut of emotions. Ranging from irritation to a stupid kind of hope, they were then followed by despair as past images rose up to mock her.

Damn the man! she thought savagely. She could do

without the caring he'd shown. Telling her that he was worried about her didn't really mean anything, did it? If it did he wouldn't have dropped her at the New Barling surgery with such a sour look on his face. When he'd eventually driven off with nothing more than a casual wave she'd felt a desperate kind of hurt deep inside.

The next morning, after checking that Mary Kolinski was on her way to the Browns' house, Kate found a waiting room packed mostly with adult patients from her lists. After seeing nothing more serious than coughs and colds they could have dealt with themselves, she realised that what most of them were really suffering from was curiosity about their new doctor.

So much for being new and also a woman, she thought as she saw the last person out at lunchtime. Yet she would rather have it that way than see no patients at all. At least they filled her mind.

As she tidied her desk, planning to nip out to the café in New Barling for a sandwich, she relived that night of agony. So, what would you have done if he'd actually lingered? a voice in her head asked suddenly.

'I'd probably have run a mile!' she exclaimed aloud. Then she felt like an utter fool as June Cranworth walked in and apologised for interrupting her as she peered around, obviously expecting to see the person to whom Kate was talking.

'You're not interrupting a thing so don't worry,' Kate said wearily. 'Just talking to myself!'

'Do you often do that?' June asked with a grin.

'Only when I'm tired. Like now. I could really do with catching up on some sleep.'

'Why don't you? Nobody's rung through for a visit, and you haven't been here long enough to gather any regulars. Take my advice and get your head down this afternoon.'

Kate handed June the current folders. 'I can't. I promised to pop in on Charlie Webb, that measles kid I saw yesterday. I said I'd visit him later in the week but I may as well go this afternoon. Just to see if his mum's carrying out all the instructions properly. She's a first-class worrier, poor woman. You never know, she might be smothering him with too much love by this time.'

June gave a little laugh. 'I really don't know how you doctors do it. Giving out all the time, yet managing to hold on to your sanity. My job's just to sort out names and put them on lists. It's much better because I never get really involved with people. Especially like you yourself, do. If I did I'd go well and truly bonkers!'

'So, what's so special about me?'

June studied her seriously for a moment. Then she said, 'Don't think I haven't noticed. I know you've only been here two minutes but that's quite long enough to see how you react to your patients. And how much they appreciate your involvement.'

'How on earth do you know all this?' Kate began to laugh, then stopped when she saw how serious June really was.

'I know because a couple of them told me. But don't overdo it, will you?'

An echo of Ben's words last night? Another warning not to become too concerned?

But how could any doctor help it? In her early years of training her professor of medicine had said much the same. But although she'd listened dutifully, trying to stay as detached as she was expected to, it just hadn't worked. There had always been some poor soul—generally a small child—who had stolen her heart. And she had always suffered with the patient as if that child had been her own.

Maybe she wasn't really fit to be a doctor, she thought. Perhaps her brothers were right to doubt her staying power.

At the door June turned to look at her, her eyes troubled. 'Please,' she said quietly, 'don't take any notice of me. I really admire what you're doing. And if you get too tied up with people—so what? It's better than not caring, isn't it? It's not every doctor who has your dedication.'

'In this practice, you mean?'

June hesitated for a moment, then she said, 'I think I'd better leave you to work that one out for yourself.'

Kate wondered of whom she was thinking. She couldn't imagine any of the doctors here being positively uncaring. Even the brash John Smith wouldn't fit into that category, would he? Then she remembered what the young doctor had said about leaving his last practice, and had her doubts. But she pushed the thought away. It was disloyal and made her uncomfortable.

Later, drinking coffee in the little café but skipping the sandwich, Kate decided that the sooner she visited Charlie Webb and his measles the better.

After poring over a map and finding that he lived quite near the surgery, she drove through some of the anonymous winding roads of the New Barling estate until she came to a small semi-detached house in a crescent with the improbable name of 'Maple Way'.

There wasn't a tree in sight, let alone something as glorious as a Canadian maple. As she unlatched an iron gate and walked up a path to the house Kate began to feel depressed. The Midlands had offered some dull places for people to live in but nothing quite as grey as this.

The house was overshadowed by a large depot for electrical goods and spare parts for DIY enthusiasts. As far as Kate could see the people living in the houses flanking it would get very little sunlight. And the thought of Mrs Webb, having to come to terms with her childlessness in this dull atmosphere, filled Kate with gloom.

She rang the bell and, just as if she had been watched, a woman immediately flung open the door.

She wasn't Mrs Webb, but a large, plump woman who looked far from friendly as she said, 'Yes? You wanted something?'

Kate tried to ignore her obvious bad temper and smiled. Then she looked down to see a small girl who was clinging to the woman's skirt, her face shadowed in its folds as two huge blue eyes stared up at her.

'I'm sorry. I must have the wrong house,' Kate said pleasantly. 'I'm Mrs Webb's doctor, and I. . .'

There was no time to finish before the woman barked, 'Oh, it's Joan Webb's house, all right! And I want a word with you! So you'd better come in.'

Kate couldn't imagine why this woman looked and sounded so angry but she stepped into the hallway just the same. Trying to stifle her own irritation, she said, 'How can I help you?'

'For a start you can tell Joan Webb to keep herself to herself. I will not have her Charlie playing with our Tina.

That lad's the devil himself! Slipping out of the house with all those dirty spots all over him! Passing them on to our Tina.'

'When did your daughter last see Charlie, Mrs— er. . .?'

'Peggy Judd,' the woman snapped, pushing the child away from her skirt. 'He often plays with her. Just sneaks out, more often than not. I caught him with her yesterday. And just look at that!' She was now shrieking hysterically as she pushed the small child towards Kate. 'Spots all over our Tina's face. And all because of that dratted Charlie!'

It was a wild exaggeration. As far as Kate could see there were only three small spots on the child's chin. They were faint enough to be ordinary pimples, perhaps caused by eating too much sugar, she thought. Nevertheless, she put her case on a chair and stooped down to take a closer look.

After examining the eruptions more thoroughly, she straightened up and said, 'This has nothing to do with Charlie, Mrs Judd. He has measles. And, if I'm not mistaken, your little girl is about to develop chickenpox.'

For a moment Peggy Judd was speechless, all her bombast disappearing as quickly as it had come. But Kate noticed that she didn't lose her underlying anger. For as soon as the woman found her voice again she embarked on a long diatribe about cleanliness, folk who didn't seem to know the first thing about illness and how sick people ought to be whipped if they couldn't behave.

'I'm sorry but I don't really understand what you're saying, Mrs Judd,' Kate said, now desperately trying to hold on to her patience. 'What has all this got to do with Charlie and his mother?'

'I'm telling you I won't have him near our Tina! His mother's got no sense. Just because she owns her house, instead of renting it like we do, she thinks that gives her the right to do anything. Like letting the lad roam about in that state. Now Tina will end up with measles as well as this chickenpox you say she's getting, won't she?'

'Or Mrs Webb's son could catch chickenpox from your Tina,' Kate said severely. 'Have you thought of that?'

This silenced the woman for a moment. Then she said sulkily, 'Well, you just tell that hoity-toity Joan Webb to keep her lad under control, will you?'

During all this time there had been no sign of Mrs Webb, and Kate found this strange. Charlie's absence she could understand because he should be in bed in a darkened room. As Mrs Judd was reaching for the doorhandle Kate asked, 'Where is your friend now?'

Mrs Judd shrugged. 'How should I know? And she's no friend of mine, I tell you.'

'So what are you doing here, then?'

'Like I said. Came to give her an earful, but couldn't find the wretched woman anywhere.'

'Have you been upstairs?'

'Not yet. Just shouted up there, then you rang the bell.'

More puzzled than ever, Kate said, 'How did you get into the house?'

'That's another thing. The silly creature leaves a key under the mat. Says it's in case her husband's lost his and she isn't in. Inviting burglars, I say!'

Kate looked at Tina. By the look of a hectic flush now spreading over her cheeks and a watery look in her eyes she seemed to be rapidly developing a raised temperature. 'I think you'd better get your daughter into bed as soon as possible,' she said quietly. 'Then phone for your own doctor.'

'Haven't got one,' Mrs Judd snapped. 'No time. We only moved in two weeks ago.'

Another unregistered patient! And one filled with unfounded self-righteousness and the temerity to criticise a neighbour for lack of care!

'Then it's high time you found one, Mrs Judd,' Kate said crisply. 'Of course, you don't have to register by law. But if you don't, and you need a doctor in a hurry, you may be charged as a private patient.'

The silence seemed to go on for ever as Mrs Judd stared at Kate, her expression turning from bad temper to doubt and then to a look of sheer admiration which spread slowly over her face. 'Well, I never!' she said at last. 'You really do seem to know your onions!'

Kate smiled as she remembered her brothers, telling her always to stand up to a bully if she wanted to see results. And that was just what Mrs Judd was, wasn't she? A bully who had now crumpled in the face of opposition.

'Who would you suggest, Doctor?' the woman asked, her voice quieter now. 'Would you take me on, p'raps?'

Would she take on a tempest that had to be overcome each time she met it? Kate looked at this woman, who seemed to have so many complications, and found herself quite liking the challenge of taming her.

'We could give it a try,' she said eventually. 'But only if you're prepared to take the advice of someone who's better qualified to deal with disease than you are.' She'd meant to leave it there but a small devil inside her suddenly made her say, 'I take it you've had no medical training yourself, Mrs Judd?'

A burst of laughter filled the little hall, and now Kate saw a real sense of humour bubbling up in the woman. She liked it, and at that moment she knew that she would be able to deal with this difficult patient without reservation.

'Cor! You're a one, and no mistake,' Mrs Judd said, opening the door and dragging the long-suffering Tina after her.

'Just wait a moment, Mrs Judd!' Kate flipped up the lid of her case and produced the documents needed for registration. 'Please fill these in and bring them to the New Barling surgery when you have time.'

'Can't I do them now and give them back to you?'

'If you like. Tell me where you live and I'll call for them.'

'I'm just next door, Doctor. But who do I say I want?'

'Well, if it's really me you wish to have as your GP then it's Dr Frinton. But there are others you might like to choose from. If you go to the surgery a receptionist will advise you.'

'It's you or no one!' the woman said staunchly, and Kate hoped that this sudden show of loyalty would last.

'Just you put Tina to bed, and I'll be in to see her when I've had a word with Mrs Webb.'

'If you're able to find her!'

'I'm sure she won't be far away. So do as I tell you now. I won't be long. And don't worry about Tina, developing measles. It's sometimes better to get them when you're a child. Saves an awful lot of bother when you're grown up.'

These words of wisdom seemed to have a profound effect on Mrs Judd for, as she left, she gave Kate the kind of look usually seen only on the face of a religious convert. Smiling to herself again, Kate went upstairs— hoping to find Mrs Webb and wondering once more why she had made no appearance while the argument had been raging in the hall.

The answer was easy. She found the woman positively cowering by the side of Charlie, who was in bed as instructed and sleeping soundly as his adoring mother stroked his forehead. When Kate reached her side Mrs Webb turned with a look of abject fear on her face.

She's been hiding up here, Kate thought, and wondered how she could make things better for the poor, sad woman.

'Has she gone, Doctor? Has that dreadful woman left?'

'She has. But, tell me, why are you so afraid of her?'

'It's simple, Doctor. She just doesn't like us, and makes no bones about letting us know. Thinks we're a cut above her or something. It's all so stupid! Wherever you come from originally, and however rich or poor you are, you're still a human being, aren't you?'

Kate studied her for a moment, then opened the pyjama top of the still-sleeping Charlie so that she could listen to his chest. 'You never said a truer word, Mrs Webb,' she murmured. 'Perhaps, given a little time, the two of you might become good neighbours, after all.'

'You really think so? I'd quite like that, you know. But it seems impossible. She's so—difficult!'

'Give her time, Mrs Webb. She's hoping to be my patient too.'

'Then let's pray we never arrive at your surgery together!'

Later that afternoon, having called on Mrs Judd and suggested that she buy calamine lotion from the chemist on the estate to help with Tina's itching spots, Kate collected the woman's registration papers and went back to the surgery to hand them in. Here she met Sheila Venables.

'Hello, there! You're just the person I was looking for,' the older doctor said, her face alight with a smile. She was large, with the slight heaviness of middle age, as well as being pleasant and friendly, with twinkling blue eyes and a smattering of grey in chestnut hair, swept up into an attractive chignon.

'So, what can I do for you?' Kate asked.

'Nothing, really. Just wanted to welcome you, my dear. I've been too tied up at The Rowans to come over before. But I promised myself to do it sooner or later. As the only other woman here, I thought you might like some female support!'

'That's kind of you.'

'It's not kind at all. I love men dearly, having been married for twenty years before I was widowed. But I must admit that I sometimes yearn to talk to another woman doctor.'

'Are you free at the moment?'

'Is one ever?' Sheila smiled knowingly, then added, 'But, if they're wise, GPs make time to talk however busy they are. I've got more than an hour before my next session at The Rowans so shall we socialise?'

'Here or at my flat? I was planning on drinking tea

and eating some sticky buns before I come back here.'

'Wonderful! My house it too far away to invite you,
I'm afraid. I live well past The Rowans, near Much
Willborough. Heard of it?'

'Only vaguely.'

'It's yet another of these picture-book villages.
Coming originally from Greater Manchester, I sometimes
think I'll never get used to them. Little groups of cottages
seem to crop up all over the place, don't they? And they
can be very isolated.'

Kate looked with new insight at this woman who could
seem so imposing. For 'isolated' read 'lonely', she
thought, pleased to find Sheila thoroughly human.

'Come on! I'll take you to my place,' she said. 'It
can't fail to cheer you up because dear old Tilly Marsden
keeps a close watch over me—and any friends I may
make! There's no chance of feeling isolated with her
around.'

'You're sure about this?'

'Of course! Only too glad, myself, to find another
woman wanting company!'

They went in Kate's car, with her promising to take
Sheila back to New Barling in good time for her to pick
up her own and drive to The Rowans for her evening
surgery. Over their tea and promised buns their conversation seemed to cover every subject under the sun. Some
of it was professional and some personal, where they got
to know each other better without ever entering the zones
which Kate always kept strictly to herself.

'So, now we've managed to introduce ourselves properly, how do you view working with me on the Well
Woman Clinic?' Sheila asked when she was almost ready

to leave. 'Would you like to consider it as a joint venture?'

'Instead of just filling in when your sessions become too demanding, you mean?'

'Yes. We could run two surgeries at the same time. Have our own separate list of patients but keep in close touch with each other.'

The idea appealed to Kate, but she saw a very obvious stumbling block and said immediately, 'I should warn you that I'm not specialised in obstetrics, Sheila.'

'But you've studied gynaecology?'

'In my general training, yes, but for the most part dealing only with straightforward pregnancies. I did go on to do midwifery, though. I also have enough knowledge to recognise gynae patients in need of referral to a specialist.'

'As far as I'm concerned, that's quite enough. You may not realise it yet but you have an ex-specialist on your own doorstep. So you really have nothing to fear.'

'Who do you mean?'

'Me, of course! I was once part of an obstetric team in a hospital up north. Enjoyed the work tremendously. But in the end I decided that it wasn't really for me so I gave it up to take a post as a GP, for which I was also qualified.' She paused, looking at Kate for a moment before she said, 'You seem to find all this rather surprising.'

'A little. I thought that once a specialist. . .'

'Always a specialist, eh? You're right, I suppose, but in my case things were different. I married out of the profession, you see. Into what you might call "Big Business" with a capital B. But my husband, bless him, almost killed himself with work so took early retirement.'

As Sheila paused Kate thought she seemed a little sad, and really didn't want to disturb her thoughts. But when the silence went on she said gently, 'You really don't have to tell me any more, you know.'

Sheila roused herself from what looked like a painful dream and said hastily, 'Oh, but I want to. After my husband retired there was no way I could carry on working in a frantically busy hospital so I changed direction. We moved to a quiet place on the Borders, where I joined a not-too-busy practice so that I could keep an eye on him.' She sighed. 'But a lot of good it did. Within five years he died.'

'Heart?' Kate asked quietly, and when Sheila nodded she said, 'I'm so sorry.'

'Don't be, my dear. These things pass. Eventually I decided to move here, away from all those sad memories. Now I have a new and very rewarding life.'

Kate stayed silent, knowing only too well how the hurt went on, even though it grew less intense with time.

After a moment Sheila looked at her watch. 'My goodness, it's getting late. I'll really have to go, if you don't mind driving me to my car,' she said. 'And, please— don't make up your mind in a hurry over the clinic. I can wait.'

'I'd like to join you one Wednesday evening, if I may, before making up my mind about running a second surgery.'

'Of course. Not this week, though. I'm closing the clinic to attend an evening seminar in Exeter. A bid to keep myself up to date, would you believe? But any other time you'll be most welcome.'

After Kate had taken Sheila Venables back to her car in New Barling she found that it was almost time for her own evening surgery. Strangely, she wasn't tired any longer and put it down to the pleasant time she'd spent with the woman doctor.

Her list this evening was smaller than usual. Yet, even so, it was dark by the time she arrived home.

Just as she was finishing supper she heard her front doorbell ring and hurried downstairs. As she opened the door she stared in surprise. It was Ben Alloway, standing there, an anxious frown on his face.

'Thank God you're here!' he said urgently. 'You're just the person I need at this moment.'

Before she could come out with the questions racing around her brain he told her that he'd been called out to an accident on the main road to Tanwyth, and wanted her to come with him in his car.

'Right!' she said, racing upstairs to get her anorak and medical case. Then she hurried to join him outside.

Sitting beside him as he drove, she asked, 'Why did you call for me and not one of the others?'

'Simple! Maurice is too old for such excitement, Sheila's too far away and John's too elusive. You're the only one available at the moment.' He paused. Turning briefly to look at her, he said, 'Besides, it's you I want with me. Especially you.'

CHAPTER SEVEN

BLUE lights from two patrol cars were flashing, and beneath the glow of the streetlamps Kate could see a group of people huddled at the side of the main road leading into Tanwyth. One police officer was holding them back as a second tried to prevent more curious stragglers from wandering to the scene. A third officer was kneeling over what looked like a bundle of clothes, while a fourth directed vehicles in single file past a badly smashed Volvo.

As Ben stopped by a temporary barrier Kate leant forward, straining her eyes to take in as much as she could. A floodlight, set up at the far end of the accident, was now switched on and suddenly everything became starkly clear. The whole scene was horrific.

Seeing the sign DOCTOR ON CALL attached to Ben's windscreen, the officer directing traffic waved them past the barrier to an empty parking space. The moment they stopped Ben grabbed both medical cases, handed one to Kate and ran from the car, leaving her to follow. In a flash she was pounding after him.

Now everything looked even more terrible to her. The tarmac was streaked with blood, and she saw that what at first had seemed like a pile of rags was actually clothing, covering a youngish man.

The officer kneeling there stood up, then stepped back to give Kate and Ben room. Stooping down to take a closer look, Kate realised that she had been mistaken about the victim's age. He was not even an adult—just a kid in his early teens. His dirty blue jeans were badly torn, with congealed blood clinging to the edges of gaping holes.

Kate suspected fractures of his shins—the tibia and, possibly, fibula in both legs. She also saw bruises on his face and a long gash on his forehead. Heaven only knew how many other injuries he had sustained, she thought, and continued to look at him in silence.

He was lying so absolutely still that there seemed to be no life left in him. None at all, she thought. And she felt a hard lump rising in her throat as she watched for even the smallest trace of movement. But she saw nothing. He gave no signs of feeling pain, and she was almost sure now that he was dead.

The despair that always came to her when she faced such tragic waste of young life rose in her with a taste of nausea. She could hardly bring herself to examine him. Yet she knew that she and Ben must both do this then verify their findings with each other, before writing their reports.

She turned to Ben who was now rummaging in his case. 'Shall I go first?' she asked, her voice husky.

He looked up quickly. 'You're sure? I'll do it if you don't feel up to it yet.'

'No, I must.'

She saw a smile touching his mobile mouth and found it reassuring. 'Just promise me you'll stop if it all becomes too much. Take it easy, Katie.'

The understanding in his voice and the way he spoke her name like that filled her with warmth, and as a kind of courage came to her she gave him a faint smile. After opening her case and pulling on surgical gloves, she turned back to the boy.

By instinct her first action was to feel for a pulse, although she was certain she would find none. But as she gently touched the base of the boy's neck, seeking the carotid artery, she became aware of a tiny flutter of movement there. It was weak, but if something was done quickly she knew that it could grow stronger, and at last hope began to stir in her.

'Not dead, but unconscious,' she murmured, giving way to Ben who was now also wearing surgical gloves as he waited with his stethoscope ready.

Standing, she turned to the man who had been kneeling beside the victim and said, 'How did he get here? He's so far from the car.' Then, fearing that more damage might have been done by inexpert hands, she asked sharply, 'Did someone lift him out?'

'I'm sorry, but I can't tell you, Doctor,' the officer said. 'He was lying here like this when we arrived. My guess is that the driver's door swung open on impact and he fell out.'

That seemed a reasonable explanation, she thought. One door was gaping wide, hanging awkwardly by a single hinge. 'Have you any idea when the accident happened?' she asked.

'Not really, Doctor. We arrived about fifteen minutes ago but I can't give you the exact time of the crash. I'm told it was a man who rang in, but he sounded too shocked to say anything coherent.'

'Of course you've sent for an ambulance?' As the

officer nodded Kate looked around then asked in surprise, 'So where is the other car?'

'There wasn't one. This was the only vehicle we found. It must have skidded into that lamp standard over there and ended up on the wrong side of the road.'

Ben was now cleaning the victim's face gently, using cotton wool dipped in the sterile water he always carried. He also had various painkillers with him, to be given by injection. But Kate knew that he would not be able to use these while the patient was still unconscious. If he was concussed injections could do more harm than good.

'Have you spoken to the man who found him, Officer? The one who rang the station?' Ben asked, then added, 'If it's OK with you, I'd like a word with him. Every bit of information helps in these cases.'

'No can do, I'm afraid. By the time we got here he had scarpered.'

'But he must be a witness, for heaven's sake!' Ben's voice was terse—filled with despair. In the floodlight Kate saw a raw kind of anger mixed with sadness in his eyes, and felt her heart aching for him.

'We don't really know if he actually saw the accident, sir. He could have found things like this. Even some time after the actual crash.'

Another team of men then appeared in a van. Jumping out with a variety of instruments, they began to measure the road. Immediately after this Kate heard an ambulance siren.

'Thank God for paramedics!' she muttered fervently. Telling Ben that she would leave him to carry on, she went to meet them.

As always, the first thing they asked for was the

victim's name. In her early days of medicine Kate had found this routine utterly incongruous, but soon came to realise how important it really was—not only for the team's records but also for the victim. Speaking a name aloud could give a great sense of safety, turning the patient into an individual who realised that help had now become something personal.

But this time the routine was useless, of course, because the lad had still shown no signs of stirring.

'We don't know who he is,' she said to one of the paramedics, who was wheeling a stretcher he had lifted from the ambulance while another was rushing to the scene with a drip held above his head.

'Then we'd better ape our American cousins,' the man said, grinning cheerfully despite the ugly scene that lay around him. 'We'll call him John Doe, shall we?'

Once the lad was strapped to the stretcher with the drip attached to him Kate followed both men as they took him back to the ambulance. Now wearing a neck brace to protect him from further damage, he suddenly opened his eyes and stared straight at Kate. He made some sort of sound and Kate leant nearer, trying to make sense of what seemed vaguely like words. A moment later she turned to the paramedic with a faint smile.

'You weren't far off the mark,' she said. 'The young man's just told me that he really is called John. He didn't mention a surname, so I guess "Doe" will have to do for the present.'

Now Ben appeared at her side. 'Would you like to go in the ambulance with him?' he asked. 'I've arranged for them to take him to Plymouth.'

'You're sure you don't want to be with him when he gets there?'

'I will be, don't you worry. I'll follow on in the car then you'll have some transport back to Lanbury.'

'Thanks. Have you had time to make out some notes for him?'

'They're already with the ambulance driver. I've also spoken on my mobile to a senior registrar in Plymouth. I don't suppose Maurice has given you your phone yet, has he?' Kate shook her head. 'Then I'll put a bomb behind him as soon as possible.'

The rest of the night seemed to just seep away, and when dawn broke at last Kate and Ben were still in Plymouth. As she had suspected, the bones in both of the boy's shins were badly smashed. As soon as he had been brought in 'John Doe' had lost what little consciousness he had gained earlier.

Two of the police officers were also there, trying to make sense of a traffic accident that had happened with no other car involved.

At last, satisfied that the boy was in the best possible hands—and leaving the police to find out who he really was so that they could contact his family—Ben led Kate to his car and drove her home to her flat.

Standing beside her as she fumbled with her key, he took it from her gently and unlocked her door. 'Will you be OK if I leave you now?' he asked. 'I'm sorry, but I must go. They will be waiting for me at home.'

'*They*?' Kate asked, before she could stop herself.

She saw him frown in the early morning light and wondered why he looked so confused. 'Well—what I really meant to say was that my housekeeper will be waiting for me,' he said. 'She's always anxious when I'm called out, poor soul. Feels obliged to be ready with hot drinks and anything else she can force down me.'

Kate said nothing. Whoever looked after him seemed to treat him like a small boy who needed feeding up, for heaven's sake! But he still hadn't really explained his slip of the tongue, had he? Maybe some other woman was also living there, she thought, and felt a kind of breathlessness she could scarcely control.

'How far away do you live?' she asked suddenly.

'Why do you ask?'

She shrugged. 'No reason,' she said, wishing that she hadn't voiced such a stupid, meaningless question. 'I just wondered if it would take you long to get home.'

He grinned at her, narrowing his eyes like some actor in a Victorian melodrama as he said mysteriously, 'My house is hidden away in an enchanted wood. Like something in a fairy-tale, it's quite a secret place.' Then he added sharply, 'And that's the way I like to keep it.'

She looked at him in silence, recognising this as a rebuff and feeling hurt because of it. She told herself to behave like an adult instead of some stupid kind of teenager.

'Well, I'd better go in,' she said at last. 'Otherwise I'll be fit for nothing when surgery time comes round. So I'll say goodnight. See you tomorrow, I expect.'

'You mean today, don't you?' Ben laughed softly, then murmured, 'Please try to get some sleep. And, Kate— don't spend too much time worrying about the lad. What you did for him was fine. Now all we have to do is wait and see.'

He stood for a moment, staring at her with those dark blue eyes growing even darker as she looked up at him. And then, as if he just couldn't help himself, he leant towards her and dropped a kiss on her cheek. 'Thanks for everything,' he said.

A moment later he was driving away as swiftly as if the devil himself were urging him on.

After only four hours' sleep Kate woke to the shrill ringing of the telephone by her bed, and reached out for the receiver. She automatically glanced at her alarm clock, panicked when she realised that she hadn't set it and relaxed as she saw that it was only half past seven.

'Dr Frinton here,' she said. Then, hearing her voice groggy with sleep, she cleared her throat and asked, 'How can I help you?'

She heard a familiar chuckle which could only belong to Maurice Gilmore. 'I'm calling to ask how you are after your disturbed night, my dear,' he said.

Kate was puzzled. 'How did you know about that?'

He gave another chuckle and said, 'A little bird told me.'

'You mean Ben Alloway, I suppose.'

'No. Although I've also been in touch with him, telling him to stay put until his tired brain gets into gear. Actually, I heard about it from the hospital in Plymouth when they rang me a short time ago.'

'I see. So what did they say to you?'

'Apart from telling me about the very hectic night you and Ben had, the doctors there were full of praise for the pair of you. Told me everything you'd done was first class.'

'What else did they say?' Kate's voice was sharp as a sudden feeling of foreboding filled her.

'Well. . .' he began. As Kate waited for him to continue her sense of unease grew out of all proportion. At last he said, 'I don't really want to tell you all this over the phone, my dear, so would you be agreeable to me coming round to your flat?'

'When?'

'In about an hour? Though I'd really like to make it sooner, if possible.'

Kate ran a hand through her hair. It was tousled and dirty after last night. And she herself felt stale. 'Why not give me time to shower and dress?' she suggested. 'And you needn't come here. I'll drive over to The Rowans. There will still be plenty of time to get back to New Barling for my morning surgery.'

'Oh, shower, by all means. But get into a dressing-gown or something. Then, after we've talked, you can go back to bed again. I've already rearranged your morning session so that you can catch up on some sleep.'

'I don't need any,' she protested. 'And certainly not if it means disrupting things like this.'

'Now, you just listen to me, young lady!' Maurice Gilmore began to sound stern. 'Take an old doctor's advice, will you? If I say you need time off I mean it. What's more, I expect you to do as I say.'

There was absolutely no answer to this so Kate gave in. 'All right—you win,' she said. 'I'll see you here in about half an hour.'

'With coffee?'

'With coffee,' she agreed. With a chuckle not unlike his own, she rang off.

As promised, she was quite ready for him. But when she invited him into her sitting room that sense of doom came back to her again. After pouring two cups of coffee she sat in an easy chair opposite him and, smoothing the skirts of her bathrobe over her knees, she felt herself growing stiff with nerves as she waited to hear what he'd come all this way to tell her.

She hoped he would come straight to the point but he took some time, stirring sugar into his coffee and sipping it, before he said, 'This is nice. Is it Dutch, by any chance?'

She nodded, trying to curb her impatience. When he still didn't say anything about last night's accident she forced herself to say, 'Yes, it is Dutch, as it happens. My favourite.'

Wondering why he was hesitating like this, she eventually realised that he was finding it difficult to speak to her, and this increased the fear growing inside her. At last she said quietly, 'What is it, Doctor? Has—something happened to that lad in hospital? Something I don't already know?'

He sighed, placed his cup on his saucer, then balanced them carefully on a small table beside him. 'Yes, my dear,' he said at last. 'This was what I almost said over the phone and then found I couldn't. It's much better that I should face you with it.'

'You mean he's—dead?'

'I'm afraid so, Kate. The young lad everyone was calling "John Doe" died very early this morning. Soon after you left Plymouth, in fact.'

So her terrible premonition had been right!

'I'm sorry,' she said quietly, trying hard to stem the

tears burning in her eyes and trying also to control a rush of anger which was surging deep inside her.

Even so, her mind kept screaming silently, What a waste of life! Over and over again she heard those words, and clenched her hands together to stop her anger growing.

She became aware of Maurice watching her so she suddenly turned her head away, blinking furiously on her tears.

At last he leant towards her, resting a hand lightly on her arm as he said softly, 'When I tell you what was said about the lad I think—I hope—it will bring you some relief, my dear.'

'Please go on,' she said, her voice hardly more than a whisper.

'Apart from the leg injuries, his skull was damaged. A really tip-top brain surgeon was called in but in the end even he was unable to save the boy. The injuries to the skull, which had seemed containable in the beginning, were found to be more extensive under a second and third X-ray. It seems that, apart from the damage noticed at first, there were also a number of other small fractures.' He frowned, suddenly looking puzzled. 'It's very strange, Kate, but some of them were found to be quite old. As if this sort of thing had happened before.'

'Another car accident, you mean?'

Maurice hesitated. 'Not really. His skull was found to be extraordinarily thin, and I'm afraid the medical staff in Plymouth suspect that these other, half-healed fractures could have been caused by a number of blows to the head. Perhaps even by someone's hand, slapping the lad too heavily.'

'Oh, my God! So what does this really mean?'

Maurice stared hard at her for a while. Then he said, 'It means that the police are now chasing up possible abuse of some kind.'

'Then—the whole thing could be manslaughter,' Kate said.

'Not necessarily. What happened previously didn't help, of course. But the real cause of death was the accident. These new fractures were difficult to deal with. In the end a minute piece of bone touched the brain and caused a haemorrhage which eventually led to death.'

'So you're really saying it was inevitable?'

'Yes, I'm afraid so. Even if the boy had lived the surgeon told me that he would never have enjoyed life as we know it. He would probably have spent the rest of his days in a wheelchair, unaware of his surroundings.'

'Yet when Ben and I delivered him to the hospital he seemed to be gaining strength. And just before he was taken to the ambulance he actually spoke to me! His voice was muffled, of course, but he told me his name was John.'

'Sadly, it wasn't. He must have been totally confused. By the time he was taken to X-Ray, although he was actually conscious, he was babbling and made no sense at all.'

'So who was he?'

'The police eventually discovered that he was called Billy Cartwright, and that he was a young lad from way over the moor. Only fourteen, would you believe? A joyrider, on his way to pick up a so-called friend who had dared him to steal a car.'

'And his parents?'

'Just a single mother. Unable to control him. She'd given up trying long ago, the police said.'

'Poor soul! However inadequate she might have been as a parent, she must be absolutely devastated. Do you think I should visit her?'

'No, Kate, no!' Maurice said quickly. 'You've done enough. You just can't take all the world's troubles on your shoulders like this. The woman's own GP will give her counselling. So just leave it, my dear. And I want you to stay put for a while so that you can get some rest. Just as I've told Ben.'

This sounded so like a command that Kate eventually gave in. But she wasn't happy about it. When Maurice finally left wherever she looked she could see some anonymous woman. However careless or even cruel 'John Doe's' mother might have been, she was still a human being filled with grief. The thought pulled at Kate's heart, and left her profoundly sad, even though she knew that it was unprofessional to feel like this.

She wasn't happy about her senior partner's new arrangements for her surgery sessions either. John Smith had been asked to see her patients as well as his own, while Sheila Venables was earmarked to take over Ben's patients at The Rowans for the rest of the day.

Now feeling weary, Kate stretched and yawned. At last she took the empty coffee-cups to the kitchen where she left them, soaking in a bowl, until she felt strong enough to wash them properly.

Afterwards she went to her bedroom, once more slipping between the sheets. With a sigh of weariness, mixed with frustration, she lowered her head onto the pillow and slept.

When she woke again it was quite dark, and her front doorbell was ringing. Rousing herself, she snapped on the bedside light and stared around, not able to make sense of anything for a moment. Her alarm clock registered eight, but there was no morning light outside. What the hell was happening?

Her tired brain slowly began to come alive, and now she remembered slipping into bed when it was daylight. Yesterday? Or was it today?

'Oh, my God!' she said aloud, as full memory came back to her. And with it, all the horror she had felt when Maurice had spoken to her of the boy's death.

There was more besides. Visions of carnage flashed through her mind. Pictures of a helpless lad who had virtually killed himself because of his youthful bravado. Now other thoughts also came to her. Of a mother Kate had never met. Possibly with a violent temper, lashing out at a son she couldn't control. Yet she also saw a vivid image of the woman grieving. Feeling empty because the boy she must have loved in the beginning had now gone for ever.

The bell rang again so, putting on her terry robe and some rather moth-eaten slippers, Kate at last went down the stairs to see who was there. When she opened the door her breath caught in her throat and she just stood there, staring.

'Ben!' she said at last, her voice still full of sleep. 'Why are you here? Has there been another accident?'

'No, love,' he said gently as she made way for him to

step into the hall. 'I was worried about you. Came to see if you're all right.'

'But Maurice Gilmore's already been here. Told me he'd rearranged our surgeries so we could both catch some sleep.'

He smiled at her, and she was suddenly filled with joy. She wanted to hold out her arms to him but knew that she couldn't. If she did she would destroy this moment because he would turn away from her with shuttered eyes—eyes that she knew could only see images of his dead wife.

But wasn't this impersonal touch what she wanted? Ben the colleague—Ben the professional. Never Ben the lover.

'Come here!' he murmured softly, touching her arms and pulling her gently towards him. 'You look so lost, Katie. I don't want to see that sadness in your beautiful green eyes. It just shouldn't be there.'

'But he. . .died!' She looked up at him, trembling.

'I know. But it's time for you to let go. If you don't you'll never be able to give your best to all the other young people you meet. And you wouldn't want that to happen, would you?'

She thought of Charlie Webb and Mrs Judd's Tina, two naughty scraps who filled her with warmth, and at last she managed a small smile.

'That's better,' Ben murmured, his cheek touching her hair as he clasped her to his chest. 'It's good to feel. If all doctors had only half your gift for being so human they would make this world a better place. But, Katie, please don't destroy yourself by feeling too much.' Then his lips were touching hers. Lightly, like the delicate wings of a moth.

'Thank you, Ben,' she whispered. 'You're probably the only person who really understands what goes on inside me.'

He looked down at her, smiling softly. 'Go back to bed,' he said. 'I'll see you tomorrow.'

Then he went away. Leaving her alone with her tumbling thoughts.

CHAPTER EIGHT

THE sudden and sometimes violent changes in the weather never ceased to amaze Kate. Because she had only seen Devon in summer, when the sun had turned her skin to a bronze that had very nearly matched the colour of her hair, she imagined that it would always be tranquil. Now, even though it was the middle of May, hail was lashing against her sitting room window. She peered out and saw the garden in turmoil, with clumps of flowers lying flat and the branches of trees tossing about wildly. Even the moor looked inhospitable, its distant hills and tors rapidly disappearing beneath a shroud of mist.

It was just like the squall she'd met when she'd first come to Lanbury, she thought. That day when Ben had rushed her to his car, unsettling her with a magnetism she'd sworn to fight against.

The memory made her shiver so, pulling her terry robe closer, she switched on the electric fire. And thanked God that it was Saturday, with no need to dress properly. Her name wasn't on the roster this weekend so, barring a whole series of accidents, there was little danger of her being called out. She didn't even have to go shopping because late on Friday night she'd joined the queues in Tanwyth's superstore.

She wandered into the kitchen, made toast and spread it thickly with butter and marmalade then decided to indulge herself with lashings of coffee. When everything was ready she took it on a tray to the sitting room. After breakfast she would just potter about, she thought. Tidying the flat, which she had neglected in favour of work, and doing any odd jobs that caught her eye.

Just as she finished eating the hail stopped as suddenly as it had started. At the same time her front doorbell rang.

Thinking that it was Tilly, calling for her rent, she ran downstairs, ready with an excuse for not staying to chat. But, flinging the door open, her words died and she just stood there, speechless.

'Ben!' she said at last, unnerved by his smile and those fascinating lights dancing in his dark blue eyes. 'What on earth are you doing here?'

'I've at last managed to winkle out your mobile phone,' he said, handing her a slim box. Looking strangely shy, he gave her another small parcel wrapped in brown paper. 'There's this too,' he mumbled.

She took the second packet, running her fingers over it curiously. It felt like a book.

She saw him staring at her, and wished that he wouldn't. Quite suddenly he began to laugh.

'So what's funny?' she asked irritably.

'You are.' He quirked one eyebrow at her. 'I don't think I've ever had a door opened to me by someone still in a dressing-gown at this time of day.'

She felt herself bridle. 'You think I should be dressed? For heaven's sake, Ben, it's Saturday!' She knew that she sounded ridiculously haughty but was unable to do anything about it.

Taking no notice of her mood, Ben said pleasantly, 'I thought we might go shopping together. We both seemed to enjoy it last time, if you remember.'

She did. Only too well. She also remembered many times since then when she had been shopping without him—and wished he'd been there. But she'd always managed to push this crazy idea firmly away. It was far too difficult to deal with.

At last she said shortly, 'All done. I'm sorry. I went to the superstore late last night. Anyway, I'm busy cleaning the flat.'

'I thought Tilly did that for you.'

'She does, but I like to give it an extra lick at weekends. I don't want her turning me out for living in squalor!'

She hoped he would laugh at that, but he didn't. In fact, he seemed crestfallen as he said stiffly, 'You might at least take a look at the other parcel I've given you.'

'You mean it's a present?'

'Not exactly. But if you like it then I suppose you can keep it.'

'So, what is it?'

'Why don't you open it and see?'

He sounded impatient, and she suddenly wanted to shut the door in his face. Seeing his bleak expression, she relented and told herself not to be so childish. 'Come in for a moment,' she said. 'It's still horribly cold out here.'

'Oh, I wouldn't want to interrupt your cleaning programme,' he said.

Detecting sarcasm, she glanced at him swiftly. But he seemed to be quite serious, with no trace of the sneer she expected. 'That can wait,' she said, then ran upstairs ahead of him, calling out, 'Please shut the door after you. Then give me a moment to dress.'

She was just about to fly into the bedroom when he whisked in front of her, barring her way. 'No, I won't wait while you dress! There's absolutely nothing wrong with what you're wearing. Great heavens, it covers everything! So come and sit down quietly and open the parcel.'

He sounded so severe that he surprised her into doing as she was told. Sitting on the sofa, she tried to look impassive. But inside she was seething—with anger at the way he was trying to control her, and also with other, softer feelings that she wanted to ignore.

When he planted himself firmly at her side she deliberately moved away from him, not caring whether it annoyed him or not. This was her flat, wasn't it? The only place where she could find any privacy.

She felt herself tensing. The way Ben was behaving reminded her vividly of the rows she'd had with David Lawrence when he'd tried to dominate her with harsh words, and she had eventually given in for the sake of peace. It was only when David's anger had turned to blows, and she had actually pleaded with him to forgive her, that she finally realised what kind of game he was playing.

Looking at her in triumph, he'd said, 'I love your slave mentality, darling! If you know what's good for you, keep it up.'

Now, staring at Ben with the kind of horror she had felt all that time ago, Kate said tersely, 'What gives you the right to tell me what I should or should not do?'

He looked at her in amazement. A whole range of expressions fleeted across his eyes. Utter surprise was mixed with a kind of despair she couldn't begin to understand. Then there was withdrawal, as if she had lashed out at him physically.

Eventually he said, 'Please, Kate! I don't know what's got into you—and maybe I shouldn't ask—but, whatever it is, can we forget it while you open the parcel?'

Controlled, well balanced, and now even sounding kind, she suddenly realised how unlike David he really was, and felt a fool for comparing the two men in her life. Then she sucked in her breath. Men in her life? That wasn't what she'd meant to think at all!

This man, sitting next to her on the sofa, most certainly wasn't in her life. Nor would he ever be if she had anything to do with it. She was still too bruised inside to tackle any kind of relationship, however different Ben might be.

When she didn't tear at the brown paper immediately he said softly, 'Go on, Kate! Please open it. I want to watch your face while you do.'

But even as he said those words he cursed himself. The last thing he should be doing was looking at her face. Every time he did something devastating happened deep inside him, and he felt his resolve never to tangle with her melting away.

Just like it had when he'd watched her in the superstore that time. Hadn't he sworn then never to let her get beneath his skin? There were too many complications in his life. Too many regrets. He just daren't get any closer to this lovely, vivid woman. If he did he would bring her nothing but sorrow, and surely she deserved something better than that!

This woman, with the trace of tragedy he often saw in her green eyes, was meant to find someone who could make her life perfect. And that person was certainly not himself, he thought—regretting everything that had happened to spoil his own life.

Now completely mystified by the sudden change she could see in Ben's mood, Kate at last tore the paper from the package. Then she gasped as she saw what was inside. It was a book, with Ben's name printed on the cover. Above that was the title—*A Modern Guide To Healing Herbs*.

She put the book down on the sofa then, before she fully realised what she was doing, she flung her arms around him to give him the biggest bear hug he had probably ever experienced.

'Ben! How marvellous!' she said, feeling his arms returning her hug and trying not to care that the gesture was obviously nothing more than an automatic reaction. 'And so soon! The publishers must be pleased. Otherwise they wouldn't have rushed it through like this, would they?'

He pushed her gently away from him and held her hands loosely as he looked at her, his eyes suddenly dancing with hidden laughter. 'What an impetuous woman you are,' he said quietly. 'But I must admit I like all this enthusiasm.'

'And so you should! You must feel proud of yourself. Publishers don't usually do things so quickly, do they? I remember how long it took for my father's work to appear.'

'Ah, but he wrote books of real scholarship, didn't he? This is just a kind of dabbling for the popular press,' he said—looking far too modest, she thought. 'Anyway, when we met on the moor that time everything was

almost complete. I was just adding a few extra illus-
trations to what had already gone through.'

She picked up the book again and spent some time
turning pages—admiring his skill as an artist, taking in
some of the text and then becoming absorbed by it.

Eventually she heard an amused voice say, 'Hey! I'm
still here, you know!'

She looked up quickly and suddenly found that she
couldn't drag her gaze away from his. The magic which
kept appearing in him tantalised her, and a shiver began
to run over her skin. He was so terribly dangerous, she
thought. Able to capture her feelings by merely looking
at her so that she wanted to sit here for ever—just basking
in the warmth of his eyes.

But then his face changed, and she saw gravity in him.
A moment later his hands were pulling on hers, drawing
her nearer so that his breath was warm against her cheek.

Suddenly she could hear snatches of a song in her
head, its notes beating in time to the rhythm of her heart.
It was a song of long ago, shared with David Lawrence
when she had thought that he'd loved her.

But she hadn't heard it in her head like this since he
went away. So why was she hearing it now?

'Don't!' she murmured softly. 'Please don't!'

'Why not?' Ben whispered. 'Is there someone else?'

'I've already told you there was.'

'But I mean now. Since then.'

'No. There's no one.'

'Then come here, Katie. Let me hold you. Please!'

He suddenly seemed so lonely. So lost. At that moment
her heart went out to him—just as it might to a patient
who was suffering.

But Ben was no patient, for God's sake! He was a man whose merest touch made her tremble. Whose very soul seemed to live beneath the shadows in his eyes.

And he moved her as no other man had ever done. Not even David Lawrence—the one person she had thought would last for ever.

Now she leant towards him and put her hands on his shoulders, offering him the sympathy she knew he needed. And she tried not to imagine that other scenario—where he smiled at her with love in his eyes, asking her to stay with him for always.

That was definitely not what she wanted, she thought. She tried to ignore an inner voice that contradicted her, telling her that she was lying and that Ben was the man she needed more than any other she had met.

'I know just how you feel, Ben,' she said, her voice shaking. 'It must be so hard for you without your wife.'

He stared down at her for a moment, and she could see a strange mix of emotions in his eyes again. First there was sadness, as if he were unable to stop grieving. Then, strangely, she saw regret. Finally there was anger.

She sensed it, burning in him like a fire, and it made her afraid. Not for herself but for him. And she wondered what had happened to make him look like this.

Then all these thoughts vanished from her mind as she felt his lips touching hers. No longer gentle as they had been after the death of 'John Doe' but fierce— demanding. And as his arms pulled her closer she felt his heart beating as strongly as her own.

God help me! she thought, as every defence in her died, and she offered her mouth willingly to him. When the warmth of his tongue found hers she gave a little strangled cry, knowing in the depths of her heart that she had never felt quite like this before. Not even in the David Lawrence days.

It was at that moment that every remembered image of her old lover fled from her mind. Now she knew that he had gone for ever, and was glad.

But it was also the moment when she received a shock greater than any she had ever known before.

For suddenly—and deliberately—Ben moved his lips from hers. Then his arms left her body, taking their warmth away with them. She didn't know when she had ever felt so bereft. She looked at him with an unspoken question in her eyes, knowing that they were glimmering on the edge of tears.

'I'm sorry, Kate.' His voice was gruff, like a stranger's. 'I shouldn't have thrust myself at you like this. It was unforgivable.'

She wanted to cry out, telling him how right this felt. But no words would come.

Eventually he stood, moving towards the door. And his face was stricken as he said, 'It's just not possible, my Katie. But, oh, how I wish it could be!'

'Why not, Ben? Just tell me why not! Don't you owe me that much?' Her voice was sharp with sudden anger.

He stared at her for a while then, moving back to the sofa, he sat beside her again. 'Yes, I owe you, Katie,' he said solemnly, 'but when I tell you I hope you'll understand why I must never get involved with you. Not just for my sake but for yours.'

'Go on,' she said huskily. 'Please go on.'

He took in a deep and difficult breath. Then he said, 'Something happened in the past that will haunt me for as long as I live. Now I can never reach out to anyone. I can't expect anyone to share the burden I will always have to carry around with me. You see—I was responsible for my wife's death. I killed her!'

She felt the breath leaving her body and looked at him, horrified. Then she said, 'I can't believe that, Ben. *I won't*!'

'Oh, Katie! So trusting. So very vulnerable,' he murmured, his eyes no longer able to meet hers.

'Vulnerable I may be, but I'm also tough,' Kate said, taking his hands again and shaking them so that he would be forced to listen. 'How else did I manage to get through medical school?'

'But that's different, Kate,' he said, taking his hands away. 'I'm talking about guilt and emotion. The horror of secret thoughts that haunt me because of something I did.'

'So did you take a knife to threaten your wife? Or a gun, perhaps?'

'Of course not! I merely stood by when I saw her drowning.'

Kate felt shock run through her but made herself stay silent, just waiting for him to go on.

At last he said, 'We were on holiday on the north coast of Devon. Swimming together in a little cove we'd found. It was almost deserted, that is, apart from an old man who soon left the beach. And a—young child we were teaching to swim. It was all so tranquil. Just like a picture in a brochure.'

He sighed, and Kate thought she had never seen a man look so bleak. Then his eyes darkened as he said angrily, 'Something terrible happened in that peaceful little bay.

The weather suddenly changed, as it often does on the north coast. A squall blew up out of nowhere, frothing the sea until it seemed to be boiling.

'Janice—my wife—was so near me one moment that I could have touched her. The next moment a gigantic wave hit her, knocking her under. But she was such a strong swimmer that when I saw her floundering I just thought she was fooling about, as she often did in the sea. It never once occurred to me that she could be in danger.'

Ben stopped speaking, turning his face away from her. She knew that the only way he would ever get rid of this torment was by talking. She wanted to urge him on but she stayed silent, not daring to interrupt his thoughts.

At last he said, 'I ran to the shore with the child in my arms, and left her under an overhang of rock to protect her from the storm. Then I looked back but couldn't see Janice anywhere. That was when I knew she was really in trouble. So, picking up the child again, I raced up the beach and knocked on the door of some man's house. I can't remember which of us phoned the coastguard but in the end help arrived.'

He hunched his shoulders, his eyes growing dark with memories as he said, 'After that—well, it was curtains for Janice!'

Kate saw anguish in him, and shivered. Not even when her parents had met sudden death had her brothers looked quite like this. But the terrible thing about Ben's grief was the guilt she could see lying beneath it.

Anger rose in her for everything that had happened to him and that even now was bringing him so much pain. She knew it was senseless but she couldn't control it.

And her voice shook as she said, 'You mustn't blame yourself like this, Ben. You must remember that whatever happened you did your best to save your wife.'

'I did? Then tell me why I still feel so much guilt. Janice was found eventually and, of course, there was a post mortem. Apparently she had suffered a heart attack. I was told it was inevitable. The pathologists found signs of aortic stenosis, and thought that the valve must have been partially blocked for some time. It had probably narrowed because of rheumatic fever she must have suffered when she was very young, they said. And I never knew any of this. But I should have done!'

'How could you have known, Ben? You're not a supernatural being with the power to look through flesh, for heaven's sake! You're human, with all the wonderful things that go with that. All the frailties, too.'

He made no effort to speak, and when she could no longer bear the silence she said, 'You're not unique, Ben. Hundreds of people feel guilt over something they couldn't prevent. But they get over it in time. They learn that if they don't they'll end up with a mass of neuroses. And that could mean real trouble.'

How long she stayed there, gently smoothing his hands, Kate never knew. All she was aware of was a gradual relaxing of his taut muscles. When she judged it safe to break the silence she asked, 'Is this the reason why you hide away in that secret wood you once told me about? And why you keep disappearing as soon as your surgeries finish? Why you never really socialise?'

He seemed to come back from a long and difficult journey. Then he said, 'Yes, it is, my Katie. It's also why

I've never married again. How could I expect anyone to live with my guilt?'

He stood up, abruptly turning away from her as if he couldn't bear her sympathy. She tried to understand it but it hurt her terribly. She forced herself to ignore the pain.

A moment later he was going down the stairs. She heard him open the door, then shut it behind him. Heard his footsteps growing fainter as he walked along the street.

At last there was nothing left. Only the echo of his words, spinning round her head.

And her heart seemed to freeze within her.

CHAPTER NINE

KATE never knew how she managed to get through the following weeks and keep her sanity at the same time. But she did. When Ben had left so abruptly, after describing his wife's death, a raw anger began to burn deep inside her. At times it changed into self-pity, then became an aching sadness for him because of the way he seemed to be destroying himself.

Eventually these feelings faded. Now whenever she was tempted to brood over him she threw herself into her work, concentrating on her patients until she almost dropped.

Later she began to realise that he was deliberately avoiding her. It hurt her desperately. Yet in some perverse way, it also helped. For now she gradually began to see him as a colleague instead of a potential lover. These days the only time they spoke was at the regular practice meetings, where he remained aloof then hurried home the moment the meetings ended.

When July arrived she found several new patients on her lists, most of them holiday visitors she had noticed wandering around the village. Goggle-eyed, they stared at the scenery as if they couldn't believe that such an unspoiled place still existed. 'Grockles', she thought with amusement, remembering the time she had also been given this title.

Sitting at her desk one morning, Kate riffled through

the folders of regular patients and then picked up a separate list of temporary people. The first of these was a Mrs Armitage, and when she called her in she was surprised to see a man and a small girl arriving with her.

'I hadn't realised this was a triple appointment,' Kate said pleasantly.

'It's really just for my wife. I'm only here to keep her company,' the man said. 'We're on holiday from Lancashire and didn't fancy leaving young Bessie in the boarding house so we brought her along, too. I hope that's all right.'

'Of course it is. How about your daughter playing with some toys while we talk? Would you mind if she took them into the waiting room? The staff will keep an eye on her.'

'That's fine by me!'

After the girl had chosen a teddy bear and a set of tea things Kate took her to June Cranworth in Reception, then hurried back to her new patient, asking what she could do for her.

'I've got a pain in my side, and it just won't go away,' the woman said. 'I didn't really want to bother you because it seems so trivial. But Bernard—my husband—insisted.'

'If it won't go away then it certainly isn't trivial.' Kate smiled, hoping to drive away the fear she saw in the woman's eyes. 'How long have you had this pain? And where is it exactly?'

Mrs Armitage pressed her hand to her right side, some way below the ribs. Then she suddenly winced.

'There, you see! The pain's really bad,' her husband said. 'What's causing it, Doctor?'

'I really can't say until I've looked at your wife more closely.'

Kate took the woman to the examination couch, pulled the curtains and left her to undress. When she returned her new patient was lying on the couch beneath a blanket, looking scared to death. She'd been pale when she arrived but now she seemed absolutely drained.

'Please don't worry, Mrs Armitage,' Kate said gently. 'This won't take long, and I'll try not to hurt you too much.'

She ran her fingers lightly over the patient's abdomen, then noticed her wince as she touched the appendix area. There was no operation scar here, which meant that Mrs Armitage still had that organ. But what state it might be in Kate couldn't tell at this stage so she used her stethoscope to listen for any abnormal sounds. Apart from the usual stomach rumblings, as if the woman had skipped breakfast, she could detect nothing else. It was a tricky situation. Even though the symptoms were vague she wasn't willing to risk a flare-up while the patient was so far from home.

'Have you vomited at all? Or suffered from diarrhoea or constipation recently?' Kate asked.

'Why, yes. I was terribly sick before we left home but then I felt better. That is, until last night when it all started again. But I put it down to a bug I might have picked up.'

'Were your husband and little girl also sick?'

'No. Actually, I planned to stay away from Bessie in case she caught it, too. But there's not much you can do in a boarding house, is there?'

Kate felt the tender area again, and the woman writhed

with a sudden spasm of acute pain. Now there was no doubt in Kate's mind what she should do and, asking Mrs Armitage to get dressed, she went back to her desk.

'What's wrong, Doctor?' Bernard Armitage asked as his wife joined them.

Her pallor had now given way to a hectic flush, and Kate knew there was no time to lose. 'I think your wife may have an inflamed appendix, but I'd like her to have a second opinion. Of course, this would mean going to hospital for a surgeon to examine her.'

Bernard Armitage looked stunned. 'Are you sure, Doctor?'

'Pretty well. But I'd like to have it confirmed one way or the other.'

'Can't it wait? We've only just started our holiday. And we're only here for a week.'

Kate wished she could say, yes, they could delay the second opinion—then send them off to enjoy this wonderful weather. But as she looked at Mrs Armitage, whose flush was now deepening as she wrapped her arms around her abdomen, she knew she wouldn't dare. That sort of decision could be fatal.

'I'm sorry, Mr Armitage, I just can't risk it,' Kate said.

'Please, Bernard! We must do what's best,' the woman said.

'Of course,' he said, patting her hand. 'Do what you have to, Doctor.'

He attempted a smile but it faded and Kate wanted to spend time with him, trying to reassure him, but it was out of the question. What was needed now was speed, not sympathy.

She set everything in motion immediately. Ringing the

Plymouth hospital, she got straight through to one of the surgeons she'd met when she'd been there with 'John Doe'. After talking to him briefly, she ordered an ambulance. She produced a map for Bernard so that he could drive behind the vehicle and return to his lodgings when his wife was settled.

'But—what about Bessie?' the man asked.

'The hospital said you could take her with you. They may even be able to find you both a bed for the night if you would prefer to stay there rather than come back to the boarding house.'

'Really?'

Kate smiled. 'Yes, really! Gone are the days when relatives were sent away after visiting hours. We have a lot of coming and going in this area, you know. And medical staff realise how important it is for patients to keep in close contact with their families.'

Once all this was done Kate returned the teddy bear and tea-set to the toy box, then called in her next patient. After examining more new patients and checking some of her regulars, she grabbed a cup of coffee and prepared herself for yet another onslaught.

The last person to arrive was Gordon Crisp, a vet who lived and practised at the far end of the village. A pleasant, middle-aged man, Kate had often come across him, walking his dogs on the moor, and had even joined him to clamber up High Tor and admire the view as they talked light-heartedly about the merits of vets versus doctors. But although he was on her list she had never treated him.

When he walked into her consulting room she saw

him as a welcome relief from her session of hard work, and relaxed at last.

'Hi, there, Gordon!' she said, grinning at him, then asked what she could do for him.

'Well, not much, really. I've got a stupid summer cold which I can treat with aspirin or whatever.' Avoiding her eyes, he laughed softly and said, 'I'm afraid I have a confession to make.'

'Try a priest,' she suggested, amusement bubbling up in her. 'Or Barmy Boris, if you like. I deal with sick bodies, not damaged souls.'

He lifted one eyebrow, looking like a clown. 'What a quick wit you have, my dear. It does me good.'

'Now you're flirting, and you know how I hate that. So go on. What's this so-called confession?'

'I'm really here to ask you a favour.'

'Oh? Don't tell me one of your patients would be better off with a doctor instead of a vet.'

'How did you guess? That's it exactly.'

'Go on, you rogue. Tell me all.'

'Well, as you know, I'm often asked to do something about rescued animals. Cats and dogs, mostly, who've been abandoned or treated cruelly.'

'So what has all this got to do with me?'

'Well, there's a dog desperately needing a home. And I wondered. . .'

'If any of my patients want a pet?'

'Oh, no! I wouldn't let the poor animal go to anyone I didn't know. I was really thinking of you.'

She stared at him, astounded. Then she said, 'No, Gordon. Most certainly not. I live in a flat, with no garden to call my own.'

'But you get about in that car of yours. Visiting patients. Even just driving over the moor for pleasure.'

'When I have time, yes. Though there's precious little of that left these days.'

'Oh, right. But don't tell there's no room in your car for Basil.'

'*Who?*'

'The dog. A wonderful, sweet-tempered greyhound who's been beaten from here to kingdom come. And all because he wasn't any good on the race track.'

She felt herself weakening, and actually heard her voice saying, 'Oh, the poor love! Who on earth would do a thing like that? And, for heaven's sake, where did he get that preposterous name?'

'No idea!' Gordon chuckled. 'It does sound rather grand, doesn't it? Almost royal. But it's appropriate. He really was a prince of a dog until his spirit was broken. So—what d'you say? Will you take him?'

'I'll think about it,' she said, knowing that her answer would probably be yes. Gordon was a good judge of animals. But, more than that, she liked the way he personalised them, using 'he' and 'she' instead of 'it' when he talked about them.

'Shall I bring him to your flat tonight?' he asked eagerly.

'No. Certainly not. Tilly Marsden would have a fit. If I do decide on him I'll come to your house, but I'll have to soften Tilly up first. After all, it's her furniture he'll be chewing.'

'But he won't. He's well past all that infantile behaviour.'

'And he's house-trained?'

'Presumably, though he was kept in a barn for ages. All on his own, poor thing!'

'Just stop that, Gordon! I refuse to be worn down by sentiment.'

'You want to bet?' Gordon grinned as he stood up to go. He opened the door, only to collide with someone coming in.

Kate heard a voice saying, 'Hello, there, Gordon!' and caught her breath when she realised that it was Ben's.

'I've been trying to persuade Kate to look after a greyhound for me,' Gordon said.

'And have you succeeded?'

'I hope so. She's thinking it over.'

As Gordon disappeared towards Reception Ben came into the room, looking more impersonal than Kate had ever seen him. She stared at him in silence for a moment then, taking in a wobbly breath, she said, 'I haven't seen you for so long I'd almost forgotten what you look like.'

She knew she sounded facetious but she couldn't help it. At least it covered the agony that still rose in her whenever he was near.

'That's a nice welcome, I must say!'

'It wasn't meant to be nice. I once thought we were civilised enough to meet each other without obligation, but it seems I was wrong.'

'Without obligation? You sound like some sort of sales person, handing out samples.'

'So you've also decided to be rude, have you? Is ignoring me not enough? Really, Ben! Anyone would think you were set on punishing me. And I'm sure I've done nothing to deserve that.'

He saw bitterness in her and blamed himself. He

almost rushed towards her to take her hands in his and tell her how much he really wanted her. But he didn't dare. That way lay disaster—not only for him, but for her.

At last he said, 'I'm sorry, Kate. I've had a bad morning, that's all.'

'So what's new? Most doctors do.'

He felt himself smiling, then straightened his face. Trying to stay impersonal was the only way he could deal with the warring emotions deep inside him. Otherwise they would surface, causing such havoc that it could lead to this wonderful woman's heartbreak.

When he didn't speak she asked, 'What are you doing here, Ben? Don't tell me this is a social call.'

'What? Oh—no, it isn't. I've come with a message from Maurice.'

'Why couldn't he phone?'

'There's nothing like the personal touch, he said. It's more persuasive. So I'm going round telling everyone there's an extra practice meeting today at The Rowans.'

'This afternoon?'

'No. Tonight after evening surgery. About eight, if you can manage it. Maurice thought it would be better then because it's likely to go on for some time, he said.'

'Right! Tell him I'll be there, will you?'

Ben hesitated for a moment, then said, 'Would you like me to pick you up? Save petrol, I thought.'

'No, thank you,' she said coolly, then she turned pointedly away to tidy her desk.

As it happened, Kate's plans for avoiding Ben went awry. After supper that evening her car refused to start. Eventually, leaving it in disgust, she rang Maurice to tell him that she'd be late for the meeting because she'd have to walk.

'No need to do that, my dear. Ben's come early so I'll ask him to fetch you.'

Kate felt she couldn't refuse, without appearing rude. But as she waited for Ben her mind was in torment—wondering what kind of mood he'd be in, and how she would respond to him.

When he did finally arrive he greeted her like a stranger, standing away from the front step and opening the passenger door of his car without a word. Trying to keep her temper, Kate sat beside him and stared straight ahead.

There was no need for him to be so surly, she thought. He usually had good manners so why didn't he call on them now? A little meaningless conversation would help. Even a faint smile. But there was nothing. Not even a trace of the comradeship most doctors shared.

Suddenly thinking of the return journey, she said, 'There's no need for you to bring me back. I can easily walk.'

'On your own? In the dark?'

'Of course, on my own.'

'Maurice wouldn't approve of that. Nor would I. It's not safe for a woman on her own at night, even in a village like ours. So you'll just do as you're told for once.'

Kate was shattered but stayed silent, even though she was seething. But she knew that her own bad temper wouldn't help. She would just have to put up with him—or get Sheila Venables to drop her, even though it was out of her way.

Still in silence, she followed Ben up the steps of The Rowans, waited as he unlocked the door with one of the duplicate keys all the practitioners carried and then went ahead of him to the downstairs staff room. The others had already arrived so, finding an empty chair as far away from Ben as she could, Kate took her notes from her shoulder bag and began to study them diligently— trying to shut out Ben's image, which kept getting in the way.

Maurice opened the meeting, inviting them to discuss any cases they wished to bring to his notice.

When it was Kate's turn she began with Maisie Brown, mentioning how healthy she now was.

'Ah, yes,' Maurice said, scanning through his notes. 'I see the blood tests revealed nothing more sinister than simple anaemia. What are you doing for her now, Kate?'

'Initially I gave her injections of vitamin B12 and followed this with prescribed iron tablets. She will stay on them for a while yet.'

'I see you also visit her at home regularly. Any special reason for that?'

Kate smiled. 'Not really. Although she attends our Well Woman Clinic regularly, I still like to keep an eye on her to make sure she's eating properly.'

'And the pregnancy she apparently knew nothing about?'

'Going well, Doctor. She couldn't be more pleased.'

'Good, good! Now, is there anyone else you wish to discuss before we move on?'

'I'd like some further advice about a patient we've already discussed. You may remember her—Mrs Burrows, who threw a temper tantrum some time ago.

Psychiatry was suggested before I came here, but it wasn't followed up.' Kate frowned, then said, 'I think I might now have found a physical cause for her bizarre behaviour but I just can't get hold of her.'

At this point John Smith interrupted. 'I remember her! I got absolutely nowhere with her. All that woman needs is to pull herself together,' he said harshly.

Kate was appalled, but stayed silent. Ben, who so far had not said a word, quelled the young doctor with a withering look and turned to Kate, asking what symptoms she had found.

'Just before Nurse Kolinski took her to her room to recover I noticed that her eyes were bulging and saw a swelling in her neck,' Kate said. 'I thought these symptoms might indicate Graves's disease.'

'Really?' Maurice Gilmore said. 'Have you had much experience with this condition?'

'Not really. I've met exophthalmic goitre only once, and know it's often associated with hyperactivity. But, as I've said, I haven't been able to examine Mrs Burrows more thoroughly—or refer her—because she disappeared. I phoned her at home, of course, but she flatly refused to come to the surgery.' Kate sighed. 'I haven't seen her since and that worries me.'

Maurice Gilmore gave Kate an encouraging smile and murmured, 'You did all you could, my dear. Perhaps it's time I pulled rank and examined the woman myself. Then, if necessary, I will be the one to refer her. That is, if you don't mind. There's a specialist in Exeter I know personally whose work is absolutely first class.'

Kate thanked him but decided not to mention any more cases because she'd already resolved their problems.

She'd managed to tame the abrasive Mrs Judd, who had now become firm friends with Mrs Webb—the next door neighbour she had once despised. And since Joan Webb had managed to control what Kate considered an unnatural lust for housework the two women apparently spent time together, relaxing over endless cups of tea.

When the meeting finally ended Sheila Venables left before Kate could ask her for a lift so it was Ben who took her home. He still seemed unable to communicate with her, and as streetlamps lit up his face she saw him frowning.

When he drew up outside her flat he suddenly turned to her and said, 'I'd like to come in, Kate.'

'Why?' she asked sharply. Then she shivered, moving away from him.

But he pulled her back, looking down at her in the warm glow of the dashboard light. 'We must talk,' he said. 'There's something important I have to tell you.'

'Oh?'

'Yes. Two things, really, that didn't actually come out at the meeting.'

His eyes were shadowed, as if he found it hard to speak to her. And she suddenly found the suspense more than she could bear.

'You'd better come in, then,' she said. 'I'll make some coffee.'

CHAPTER TEN

As THEY stood together on the step Kate began to feel uneasy. Inviting Ben in for coffee like this was surely the most foolish move she had ever made. The last thing she really needed was to be alone with him.

'Is this wise?' she asked breathlessly.

'What? Drinking coffee together, you mean? Quite harmless, I should have thought.'

Of course. Drinking coffee was all it meant, wasn't it?

'So what is this news that's so pressing?' she asked.

'Not here. Voices have a nasty habit of carrying at night. Let's wait until we get inside, shall we?'

She opened the door and ran upstairs ahead of him, hurrying into the kitchen. After filling the percolator with water and shaking coffee into the container, she set it on the stove, then watched him walk into the room. He now looked so preoccupied that she doubted whether he could really see her.

'So, when do I get to hear the item no one mentioned at the meeting?' she asked impatiently.

'When you're ready to face the fact that one of your colleagues will soon be leaving the area.'

How long she stood there in silence she didn't know. She was only aware of wrestling with emotion that threatened to swamp her, making her have to fight for breath. There was an icy chill deep inside her, and she didn't know how to deal with it. For, without being told, she knew exactly who he meant, and clenched her hands as she waited for him to speak his own name.

But he stayed obstinately silent. When she could bear the tension no longer she asked, 'Who is it, Ben? This person who's leaving.'

'All in good time,' he replied, with a smile that just shouldn't be there. 'Let's have coffee first, shall we?'

She wondered how he could sound so—ordinary when what he was going to tell her would shatter her. Trying not to look at him, she placed cups and saucers with milk and sugar on a tray. Asking him to bring in the coffee, she went to the sitting room, put the tray on a small table by the sofa and sat down. She felt gauche and awkward. And when he sat beside her, stretching his long legs in front of him, she felt as if her nerves would snap.

She saw him watching her silently as she poured the coffee. Sheer despair was making her hands shake but she tried to hide her clumsiness. Unwelcome thoughts began to race around her head, bringing her so much pain that she wanted to cry out with it.

How would she manage when he left? What would she do when this tall giant of a man took away the wonderful gentleness that was such an integral part of him? All the moods and anger, too. Yes, she would even miss those, she thought miserably.

Quite suddenly she saw an image of a strange house, surrounded by woods. Because she had never actually seen it the house remained shadowed and mysterious. But she knew that it was beautiful, and found herself wishing that she could live in it with Ben.

With an effort, she finally managed to push these thoughts away. They were dangerous. Obsessive. And this was the last thing she needed. She had been obsessed once before with a doctor who had made her feel special. And who had walked out of her life because she wasn't willing to meet his terms.

'Why so thoughtful?' Ben asked, his cup halfway to his lips.

'Nothing special,' she lied.

'Are you now ready to hear the news I promised?'

She bit her lower lip, suddenly wanting to scream at him. To tell him that he was a fool to even think of leaving Lanbury and that no way could the practice manage without him.

'Yes, of course I'm ready,' she said, knowing that she would never be.

She saw his lips move but was unable to hear what he said because of the words which were still storming around her head, blocking her ears.

But when he said, 'So what do you make of that?' she came back to earth with a jolt that was almost physical.

'I'm—sorry,' she murmured. 'I don't understand what you're telling me.'

He gave a gruff laugh. 'You weren't listening, were you? Your head was filled with dark, unhappy thoughts, wasn't it? For heaven's sake, tell me about them. Then get rid of them!'

The irritation she heard in his voice riled her, and she suddenly wanted him to get up and leave. Now. Even before he had drunk his coffee. She wouldn't stay here and listen to words that were sure to destroy her.

Then she heard a voice in her head telling her not to be so childish so, taking in a ragged breath, she said, 'I was wondering what it would be like here without you. How on earth—all of us would manage.'

He looked utterly astonished. Then he said, 'That just proves you weren't listening! What makes you think I'm the one who's leaving?'

'You're not? But when you first said. . .'

'As impetuous as ever! Jumping to conclusions,' he said. And a crooked smile that didn't match his severity pulled at his lips.

'I'm sorry,' she said, unable to look at him any longer. 'Being impetuous is one of my biggest faults, I'm afraid.'

'But you shouldn't be afraid, Katie. It's part of you. Something that I hope will never change because it's so delightfully honest.'

Now he was calling her Katie again, and his voice was so gentle that she could hardly bear it.

At last she managed to look at him and asked, 'Then who is this person who's leaving?'

'Two people, actually. Nurse Kolinski for one. But she's only taking six months' leave. As you probably know, her grandfather was a Pole who escaped from his country during the war and came to Britain and trained as an air pilot. He then went back to fight for the country that had been wrested from him by Adolf Hitler.'

'Did he suffer terribly during the occupation?'

'Yes. All those brave men did. But a lot of them escaped, then served the people they'd left behind by fighting from England, the country they came to call their own.'

'Blood and guts,' Mary had said. Now Kate knew why. The nurse had promised to tell her all about it one day, but they'd never managed to get round to it.

'Was Mary's grandfather Jewish?' she asked.

'No. Just one of the many rebels fighting for freedom. Now Mary thinks it's time to seek out any family who might have survived, despite all that happened to them.'

Kate sighed. 'I'll miss her dreadfully.'

Ben smiled. 'Don't worry, she'll be back. Probably with a whole string of cousins, if I know her.'

'I hope so,' Kate said. Then she asked, 'Who's the other one leaving?'

'John Smith. Our doctor who thought that everyone was spying on him.'

'And were you?'

'Yes—and no. For his own good, Maurice and I kept a close eye on him. I'm afraid we found him lacking in many ways, but not so badly that he could be asked to leave.'

'Why didn't Maurice mention him at the meeting?'

'Because John asked him not to.'

'Why exactly is he going?'

'For lots of reasons. He never really fitted in here, you know. And I think he eventually found out for himself how inadequate he was so he decided to leave before anyone suggested it.'

'Poor John! If he's appointed as a GP somewhere else I suppose this sort of thing could happen all over again.'

'Exactly. But I think he's foreseen this because he recently applied for a consultancy with a leading drugs company. What's more, he was appointed. So here's luck to him! He'll be far more suited to working behind a desk and overseeing medical products than he ever was treating people he never really understood.'

Kate stared at nothing for a while. Eventually she became aware of Ben looking closely at her, his dark blue eyes growing serious. 'What is it?' she asked, suddenly breathless.

'It's—us, Katie. We can't go on like this! Avoiding each other. Being even less than friends. I just can't stand it!'

She looked straight at him, and was suddenly unable to move her gaze away from his. Holding her breath, she watched all those changing expressions moving in his eyes again.

And before she knew what was happening she was in his arms. Just as she had been that day he'd given her his book. At that time he had kissed her, hadn't he? But she also remembered him pushing her roughly away, shattering all the tenderness that had been between them.

Now she wanted him to stay close. Despite her determination never to get entangled with any man again, she ached to stay in his arms like this for just a little while longer.

Suddenly he was kissing her again. As a lover kisses. And there was no way she could resist the softness of his lips. Her skin tingled, and her body seemed to melt as a musky scent that was all man touched her nostrils. She shivered as his hands began to roam over her breasts, making the nipples spring up with a will of their own.

Now his fingers were burrowing beneath her clothes, slipping the catch of her bra, unleashing her. And she drew in a sharp breath as the coolness of his fingers touched her naked skin. When his mouth left hers to suck at the tautness of her breasts she moaned with an exquisite sense of pleasure.

At last he moved his lips away from her body, and she felt as alone as if he had just walked out of the room.

He was rejecting her again, wasn't he? Something was warning him not to get involved. Soon she would be left with nothing but the tears she dared not shed in front of him. Yearning for something she would never reach.

She sighed. She and Ben were just not meant to come together, were they? They were both too chained to the past to find the freedom to love again.

She stirred in his arms, wanting to leave the warmth of them before she was tempted to stay there for ever. Soon he would be driving to his own home—wherever that was.

With a feeling of desperation she tried to balance her thoughts. One day, she told herself silently, she would be able to look back and recognise this time for what it really was. Nothing more than a healing of their differences. A softening of their edges so that the awkwardness between them would go away.

If she could see it like that she knew that this dreadful yearning deep inside her would eventually disappear.

She tried to move right away from him but his arms suddenly tightened around her. 'Where do you think you're going?' he asked quietly.

Stunned for a moment, she could find no voice. When she did manage to speak at last she sounded shaky and breathless. 'I was going to let you out,' she said, then added stupidly, 'Unless you want more coffee, of course.'

'I don't.' His own voice was now hoarse and strained. 'I just want you. So badly I can hardly bear it.'

She stared at him in silence. Understanding—yet trying not to. Before she could speak again he began to smother her face with kisses, his lips touching her skin like the soft drift of feathers. Then his tongue was tickling the lobes of her ears, before his teeth gently nipped their flesh, bringing her an exquisite kind of agony that did not really hurt at all.

At last his lips met hers again, and the room no longer existed for her. She was outside her body, flying up into a sky that was filled with dreams.

But the dreams began to dissolve as she thought, This mustn't happen to me. Nor to this man because he belongs to someone else.

And she remembered the time when he had hurried home, telling her that 'they' would be waiting for him. A slip of the tongue she'd thought, trying to believe it. But she never had. Ever since that time she had pictured two people who lived with him. One was the house-keeper. The other was a mystery who, in her imagination, gradually turned into a young and very beautiful woman. Why else would he hide himself away in that damned wood?

Now anger spurted in her. Whether that other person really existed or not made no difference. Ben was still not free. Whatever happened to him the phantom of his dead wife would always be with him, living in his mind like some ghost intent on destroying him.

As she tried to pull away from him again she found herself looking into a pair of dark blue eyes that seemed to be burning right into her.

'Ben?' she asked hopelessly. 'What are we doing?'

Instead of the regret she expected to see in him as he rejected her once more, she found herself looking at a face that was softened by pleasure. Then she heard just the trace of a laugh before he murmured, 'I thought we were kissing each other.'

'But—we shouldn't be.'

'Why not?'

Had he forgotten how he'd pushed her away that last time? 'Because you told me it was—not possible,' she said huskily.

A shadow passed over his eyes, turning them almost black. 'I know,' he said softly, 'but somehow I can't come to terms with that. It gives me so much—agony. I need you, Katie. I need you so badly.'

Desperate. Pleading. How could she deny him?

He hadn't spoken of love—only of need. And she told herself to be thankful for that because she knew she just couldn't face his love.

She was adult enough to understand what he wanted, and knew the sort of torture a man could suffer when he was stirred physically by a woman. And, for heaven's sake, she also had needs, hadn't she? Desires that were as real and as pressing as his own.

The strength of him, which mingled so naturally with the sweetness of his compassion, pulled at her resistance until it began to disintegrate, then finally just floated away.

She looked at him in silence for a while. Then she spoke his name. Nothing more.

'Ben?' she said, turning the word into a question. The sound of her voice seemed to hang on the air.

Then he was picking her up, carefully cradling her in his arms as he walked slowly towards her bedroom.

Some time in the night Kate heard Ben stir and reached out her hand to him. But her bed was empty.

She snapped on the light, looking for him. Then her

body grew stiff as she saw him standing with his back towards her, pulling on his clothes.

'Where are you going, Ben?' she asked. And as he turned to face her in the warm glow of the lamplight a feeling of panic rose in her.

'I'm sorry! I didn't mean to wake you,' he said.

'Has there been a call I slept through?'

'No, Katie. It's just that I have to go home.'

A shaft of anger suddenly stabbed at her, killing the magic they had known together. 'Why now?' she asked, her voice sharp and ragged. 'For God's sake, Ben! It's still dark.'

'I'm going because I have to,' he said, suddenly irritable. 'Surely you can understand that?'

She couldn't. Not now, after they had shared so much. The gentle touching that had grown into a fierce moulding of body to body. His sexual arousal that had pulled at her own until she had offered herself freely to him.

During the night, when she had lain listening to him breathing, a kind of wonder had crept over her. It had all seemed so perfect. She knew he hadn't been looking for love. But when he took her to the highest peaks she could have sworn she had glimpsed his soul.

Had he felt nothing? Nothing at all but physical passion? Were his eyes still so full of his dead wife that he hadn't even seen the woman he was really making love to?

Now she waited for him to reject her, telling her again how everything was impossible.

A deep anger stirred in her, and she clutched at his hand. 'Don't go, Ben! Stay with me.'

'I can't. You know very well I have to go.'

Bitterness welled up in her. 'You've used me, Ben,' she said huskily. 'Any stranger would have done for you tonight. So why did it have to be me?'

She expected him to turn away with an anger that matched her own. But he didn't. Strangely, he was looking at her with a deep sadness in his eyes. Then he sat on the edge of the bed, just staring at her. After a while he leant towards her, cupping her face in his hands as he kissed her gently on the lips.

'Please, Katie. Don't hate me like this,' he said. 'I might deserve it—for destroying your privacy. But I didn't use you. You'll never know just how much you have done for me. How you've restored my faith in life again.'

Then he went away, his feet so silent that she could hardly hear him going down the stairs. And she was left alone with an echo of his words. Words that haunted her. And would continue to haunt her because she just couldn't push them away.

But she knew that she must—if she was ever to find any peace again.

CHAPTER ELEVEN

KATE found Basil absolutely irresistible. The moment she saw the dog in Gordon Crisp's garden she fell hopelessly in love.

'Oh, you lovely, lovely creature,' she murmured, kneeling on the lawn as she patted his head and felt the silkiness of his ears. He lifted his face to her, and she found herself looking into a pair of limpid brown eyes. Then she smiled at him, and his mouth opened, his tongue lolling as he panted at her. Just as if he understood how much she loved him, she thought.

Oh, yes, he was perfect. Thin and scrawny because of the terrible things that had happened to him, of course. But, nevertheless, wonderful.

When she felt a warm tongue licking her hand she looked up at Gordon and said, 'I really came to tell you I couldn't possibly take him. Even though Tilly said she wouldn't mind.'

'So I suppose that's it, then.' Gordon sounded disappointed.

'Not at all! I've changed my mind.'

'Since when?' he asked, giving her an impish grin.

'Since just now. You really are a rogue, Gordon! You knew I'd go all soppy the moment I saw him, didn't you?'

'Let's hope it's not just a passing affair, then.'

She laughed. 'I don't approve of affairs.'

'I see,' he said gravely. 'So you're the sort of woman who's faithful, are you?'

'As far as animals are concerned, yes.'

'And people?'

She snatched in a quick breath. 'That's another matter. One I'd rather not discuss, if you don't mind.'

'Of course! Sorry, I didn't mean to pry. So, where do we go from here?'

'I'll take Basil home with me now. Then go straight to the best pet shop I can find in Tanwyth. Buy lots of dog food, a basket and lead, and a good blanket for him to sleep on.'

'No need.' Gordon squatted beside her, stroking the dog's neck. 'He's got those things already.'

'Then I must pay you for them. For the dog, too.'

'That you won't! A contribution to an animal charity will be quite enough.'

'You're too kind to me,' she said.

'Oh, none of this generosity is for you, young lady. It's for the dog.'

Kate laughed and then, thanking him as he put the things he'd given her into the boot, she snapped a lead onto Basil's collar and helped him into the car.

Sitting in the passenger seat and looking thoroughly regal, the dog behaved beautifully all the way home. When Kate unlocked the door to her flat he walked with great dignity up the stairs, trotted round to inspect all the rooms then plonked himself on Kate's bed.

'No, you don't! I'm starting as I mean to go on,' she said, gently patting his rump. 'It's the kitchen for you, my lad. And you'll sleep there in your basket, if you don't mind.'

But Basil did mind. Turning his back on the kitchen, he made a beeline for the sitting room, sprawled in front of the fireplace and refused to be budged. In the end Kate took his basket in there, then laughed to herself at the dog's strength and her own weakness. He looked up at her with his head on one side. Just as if he was thinking over what she'd said to him, Kate thought. Then he gave one solitary bark, before snuggling down in his bedding and staring at her with a great deal of love in his eyes.

'So you approve of me, do you? I can't tell you how happy that makes me,' she said.

She didn't feel in the least foolish, talking to the dog like this. It was almost like having another person in the flat, she thought. And it certainly took away some of the agony that had lodged inside her since Ben had left her so abruptly after they had made love.

Apart from practice meetings, where he said very little before hurrying away, Kate had had no real contact with Ben since that night. He now seemed to be deliberately avoiding her. But she couldn't blame him. Not after she'd been so angry with him.

Fortunately, she was too busy treating patients to brood too long over him, and spent every spare moment she had walking Basil over the moor. She also took the dog to the surgery if she knew she would be home late. Here he spent most of the time sleeping in Reception, with June feeding him forbidden titbits. When she made house calls she took him with her, and he sat peacefully in the car while she visited patients.

When the time came for Mary Kolinski to leave the staff threw a party for her in Maurice's drawing room at The Rowans. It was here that Kate at last came face to face with Ben. But, even so, there was no time for more than a casual greeting, for immediately after he had sampled the cake made by the staff he was off again.

When it was John Smith's turn for a leaving party the young doctor chose New Barling as the venue. Here Ben turned up again, and actually smiled at her as he caught sight of Basil.

'I see you let Gordon persuade you in the end,' he said. 'Not many people can resist that man's blackmail!' Then he hurried away again, as if there wasn't a moment to lose.

These days Kate was thankful for her patients, and found great satisfaction in following up their cases. Mrs Armitage finally left hospital to go back to Lancashire—but not without leaving a thank-you card in Reception. Most of Kate's young patients who had succumbed to measles were now in the best of health—Charlie Webb among them. Even Mrs Judd's small daughter, whom Kate still thought of as 'our Tina', had managed to recover from chickenpox without also contracting measles.

But what Kate found more pleasing than anything was a special visit from these two families, who had once quarrelled bitterly. Just as her last patient left at lunchtime one day both mothers arrived with their children. After smiling shyly, they presented Kate with a huge bouquet she was sure they couldn't really afford.

'What on earth have I done to deserve this?' she asked, running water into a vase then setting the flowers on her desk.

'Two things,' Mrs Webb said brightly. 'You're the best doctor I've ever had, for one. And the other is—

well, you found a friend for me on that lonely estate. Now I can't think what I'd do if Peggy Judd ever moved away.'

Success indeed, Kate thought, smiling at the two women who were now hanging onto their children as if they feared the little scamps would start climbing over the furniture.

'Thank you,' she said, feeling a suspicious prickle of tears at the back of her eyes. 'It's very kind of you.' She didn't add that at one time it had been touch and go— when she had almost told them both that enough was enough.

Then there was Maisie Brown, who waddled regularly into the Well Woman Clinic for appointments she wouldn't dream of missing. She sometimes brought Joe with her, who looked more than happy these days because he'd been promoted to foreman on the building site. And he never ceased to look proud of his extra-large wife.

Even Michael Lee, of the fancy-dress dog collar, never pestered Kate seriously these days. Her sharp words had certainly done the trick, she thought, for now he never seemed to need a doctor at all!

Soon after Kate had received the bouquet from the Judds and the Webbs, Maurice Gilmore fixed a date to interview candidates for John Smith's post. Although this really had nothing to do with Kate—because she was the youngest partner—he asked her to attend.

'Ben will be with me, of course,' he said. 'And I've also asked Sheila Venables. But unfortunately she can't make it.'

'Do you really need me?' Kate asked, thinking he had only invited her out of courtesy. 'I don't want to be in the way.'

'Now you're talking nonsense!' Maurice frowned, using the severe voice that even now could make Kate quail. 'It's absolutely necessary for you to be there. Whoever's appointed will spend most of his time at New Barling with you. So you'd better vet him, hadn't you?'

'No women to choose from, then?'

'No. Only men applied. Would you rather work with a woman?'

Kate shrugged. 'I'm easy either way.'

One Sunday afternoon, the day before the interviews, Maurice called at Kate's flat. Opening the door to him, she smiled with pleasure. Then she grew serious when she noticed his worried frown.

'What's happened?' she asked quickly.

'Ben Alloway. That's what's happened! I can't get hold of him anywhere. Tomorrow's interview times have been changed and I must let him know, but he's gone to ground. His phone seems to be out of order, and he's shut his mobile down for some reason.'

'Why don't you drive to his house and talk to him there?'

'I can't, my dear. Otherwise occupied, I'm afraid. So I came to ask if you could winkle Ben out for me. Would you mind driving there with a message? I've put everything in this letter. If you go now he'll have time to rearrange any visits he's already planned.' He handed her an envelope.

'I'd go willingly,' Kate said, 'but I'm afraid I don't know where Ben lives.'

'Really?' Maurice sounded surprised. 'I know he likes

to keep his whereabouts private but I thought he would have told you by now.'

She frowned. 'Is there any particular reason why he's so secretive?'

Maurice gave her a solemn look. 'Yes, there is, my dear. But if he hasn't told you then. . .'

'Oh, I know he finds visitors difficult since his wife's death. I just wondered if there was something else that makes him shut himself away like this.'

'There is,' Maurice said, 'but I really can't betray a confidence, Kate.'

'Of course not,' she said quickly. 'But I suppose this means he won't be too pleased when I turn up.'

'It can't be helped, Kate. It's vitally important for someone to get in touch with him.'

'How about tomorrow—before his morning session at The Rowans? That will give him plenty of time to cancel afternoon visits, won't it?'

'He's not due there until the evening. He has the morning off so Sheila's standing in for him.'

Kate sighed. This was just the sort of dilemma she disliked, doing something for one person while the other would probably hate her guts for the rest of his life because of it.

In the end she took the scrap of paper Maurice offered her, with Ben's address hastily scribbled on it, and put it in her shoulder-bag with his letter. Then, still in the sundress she was wearing and with her bare feet thrust into sandals, she slipped on a lightweight cardigan, bundled Basil into the car and drove to Soo Hutton, a village she had never visited before.

It was little bigger than a hamlet, and after driving

past a handful of cottages she met open countryside again, with no sign of the house she was looking for. At last she saw a copse of gnarled and ancient trees. Ben's mysterious wood?

Parking at the side of the road, she left Basil in the car while she looked around. Eventually she saw a notice attached to a post saying HONEYWELL HOUSE. She was in the right place, but the copse was so thick that she wondered how on earth she would get through it.

Looking for a road skirting the wood, she could find nothing. Basil began to bark impatiently so she went back to him, clipped the lead to his collar, helped him out of the car then locked it.

'Come on, boy! Let's get into this jungle,' she said, making for the trees and hoping that she would eventually find a house in the middle of them.

Basil began to dance about with excitement so, giving him his head, Kate let him pull her up a grassy bank. When they reached the middle of the copse Basil decided to squat in front of a rabbit hole, obstinately refusing to move.

'Come on, you young devil! We haven't got all day!' she said, tugging on his lead until he at last stood up.

Her hair was now in a mess from tangling with low branches, and her legs were scratched by brambles. At one point the copse became so thick that most of the sunlight disappeared and she could hear soft flutterings, followed swiftly by the screech of a bird's alarm call.

It could have been the setting for a horror film, Kate thought. But, strangely, she saw it as a place of gentle magic. Walking on again, she at last came to a clearing. And there, at the far end of it, was a large house.

'Look, Basil! What do you make of that?' she said.

The dog began to prance about so she wrapped his lead round her hand, shortening it. Then she stood quite still, staring at a two-storey building of mellowed stone which glowed in the sunlight. It was gracious, with long windows surrounded by delicately carved coping, and Kate found it so beautiful that it took her breath away.

In front was a large circular lawn, surrounded by white fencing, with a small gate set into the far end of it and another on the side nearest to her. Sweeping away from the house was a gravelled drive, obviously leading to the road she had missed in her hurry to get here.

When she spotted Ben's car, parked by the front door, she cursed herself for being so utterly stupid. Not only had she scratched her legs, she'd also snagged her dress. Sighing, she stood by the little gate and tried to find the courage to go on.

Then she became aware of movement near the house. A moment later she saw a small girl, coming towards her. Kate judged her to be about eight or nine, and as the child broke into a run she noticed that her movements were awkward. Her right leg was thrusting away from her body so that she seemed to limp.

At first Kate thought she was playing a game. Pretending to be a horse, perhaps. But as the child drew nearer Kate realised that there was something physically wrong with her.

When Kate had spent time working at a hospital in the Midlands she'd sometimes come across small patients with an awkward gait like this. Most of them suffered from defective hip joints which caused pain, and also made them clumsy. Some of these children had undergone surgery, followed by post-operational exercises from a qualified physiotherapist. By the end of the treatment, instead of working in a circular motion, the leg usually moved normally. But it wasn't always the case.

As the girl loped towards the fence Kate wondered whose child she was. She was frowning now and looking fierce so Kate tried to reassure her by smiling.

When that didn't work she said, 'Hello, there!' and waited for the frown to disappear. But it didn't. By the time the girl finally reached the gate it had turned into an ugly scowl. Then her furious voice was shouting a kind of gibberish that might just be some foreign language, Kate thought.

'My, my!' Kate said cheerfully, determined not to be intimidated by the display of bad temper, in whatever language it came. 'Can you speak English?'

The child stared at her coldly with unblinking brown eyes. Then she pushed back a mass of dark curls, and with no trace of foreign accent she said, 'Go away!'

'Why? Am I spoiling some game you're playing?'

'Yes, you are!'

Basil, who had been cowering behind Kate's skirt at the sound of the child's raised voice, suddenly appeared. He gave one loud bark, before squatting on his haunches and staring at the child imperiously.

The effect on the little girl was electric. After giving Basil a startled look, she said something in that strange language, then pushed her hand through the fence and smiled as she patted his head.

'You're very brave,' Kate said. 'It's not always wise to touch a strange dog, you know. He could have bitten you.'

The child promptly withdrew her hand, leaping away from the fence. 'Horrid dog!' she said crossly. 'You can both go away!' Then she turned her back and shoved her small bottom against the gate so that Kate couldn't open it.

At that moment Basil gave a pitiful whimper, as if he understood that he was unwelcome. Then he lay down with his paws flat on the ground, looking like a slave doing penance.

'Poor Basil,' Kate murmured, thinking of all the times he must have adopted this attitude when his last owner had beaten him. Turning to the little girl, she said, 'He's been unhappy for a long time. Now he thinks you don't like him.'

Suddenly all the child's anger disappeared and she crumpled into a heap on the grass, bursting into tears.

Kate pushed against the gate, gradually managing to slide it away from the girl, who was now shuddering with sobs as she buried her face in her hands.

'Come on, my little love! I'm not going to hurt you,' Kate murmured, squatting down beside her. 'Nor is Basil.'

She reached out to stroke the tangle of dark curls, hoping to bring the poor little creature some comfort. She had no idea why the child should suddenly weep like this, but knew instinctively that it wasn't really because of the dog. No, these tears were for something else. Even if it was purely imaginary it made no difference, Kate thought. For whatever was causing all this grief was very real to the girl.

The sobbing stopped for a moment, and the child looked up at Kate. Her pale little face was now streaked with grime and tears, running in rivulets down her cheeks.

In the silence Kate decided to use an ambulance man's technique and asked, 'What's your name?'

The request was so sudden that the girl replied without thinking, just as Kate had intended. 'Pippa,' she said. 'What's yours?'

Offering her a handkerchief, Kate said seriously, 'Kathryn Wilhelmina Frinton. Most people call me Kate, or Katie. But I don't often let them know about the Wilhelmina bit because it would make them laugh.'

'Why? I think it's a nice name,' said a voice, now muffled by Kate's handkerchief.

Then the child broke into that gibberish again, and when she saw Kate's puzzled frown she laughed. 'Do you like my secret language?' she asked, holding the handkerchief to her face like a veil and peering at Kate over the top of it. Then she raised her eyebrows, trying to look seriously grown-up, Kate thought.

'It sounds absolutely wonderful to me but I'm afraid I don't understand it. So why not tell me what you just said in English?'

Now looking as mysterious as if she were the keeper of the world's biggest secret, Pippa suddenly announced, 'I write stories, you know.'

'And was this one of them?'

'Yes. It's about an old woman called Maggie Flute, who makes children dance to the music she plays. On a flute, of course. That's where her name comes from.' Pippa paused, giving Kate a hard look—as if testing her sincerity. Then, obviously getting rid of any doubts on that score, she whispered hoarsely, 'It has to be in my secret language cos it's about a real person, you see.'

Who on earth was this child? Obviously extremely intelligent, she was also highly imaginative. Secretive, too. As if she needed to hide from the world for some reason.

Kate wondered if her rapid diagnosis about the awkward walk had been correct. Was Pippa really lame? Or was that all part of a story she had invented?

Then Kate's thoughts scattered as the child suddenly pulled at her hand, demanding a story about the dog.

Kate racked her brains, desperately trying to find something to say that would amuse this strange little creature. At last she came up with, 'Well, when we were trying to find this house Basil and I got stuck in that wood over there. And I could hardly get him to follow me because he was sitting down and just wouldn't move. Can you guess why?'

'No,' Pippa said, her eyes wide with curiosity. 'Please tell me.'

'He was sitting in front of a large hole. Just waiting for a rabbit to appear.'

'And did one come out?'

'No. But poor Basil seemed so disappointed that I had to tell him he might find one next time he waited there.'

'Did he want to play with the rabbit, then?'

'Er—yes,' Kate said, hoping that the child would never know what the dog really wanted.

Now Pippa suddenly stood up. Clinging to Kate's skirt, she hid behind it and said urgently, 'She's coming! Maggie Flute is here. She's ever so fierce so you'd better watch out!'

Kate looked across the lawn to see a thin, middle-aged woman coming rapidly towards them. As soon as she was within earshot the woman shouted, 'I don't know who you are, but if you don't leave that child alone I shall report you to the police. Travellers and the like are not welcome here!'

'But I'm not a traveller,' Kate protested.

'Really? Then why are you dressed like that?' she asked, looking pointedly at Kate's ruined dress.

Basil, who had been hiding behind Kate from the moment he'd heard anger, now peered at the woman, not even doing his famous one-bark routine. She took one look at him and said, 'Coming here with a lurcher, too!'

'He's not a lurcher,' Kate said indignantly. 'He's a full-blooded greyhound.'

At that moment someone else came from the house and dashed across the grass shouting, 'Stop! Mrs Bruton, *please*!'

It was Ben. He obviously recognised her, despite her dreadful appearance.

'But this person is trespassing, Doctor,' Mrs Bruton said. 'You can't be too watchful these days.'

'Thank you for your care, my dear,' Ben said, 'but this time it's quite unnecessary. Please meet my colleague, Dr Frinton.' He introduced the woman to Kate as his housekeeper, who now unbent a little and actually managed a smile.

Pippa loped over to Ben and flung herself at him. Immediately his arms went round her small body and he picked her up, giving her a kiss before setting her down again.

Then he looked at Kate with a deep sadness in his dark blue eyes and said, 'What are you doing here, my Katie?'

Her heart leapt to hear him calling her Katie like that

and she smiled nervously, hoping that he wouldn't hate her for intruding like this. 'I've brought a message from Maurice about tomorrow's interviews. It's all in this letter.' She handed him the envelope.

'Why didn't he ring me?'

'He tried to but couldn't get through. He said your phone's out of order. And your mobile's not working either.'

'Oh, I see.' Turning to Mrs Bruton, he asked her to rustle up some refreshment.

'Oh, no, I don't want to trouble anyone,' Kate said hurriedly. 'I've delivered the message so I'll go straight back, if you don't mind.'

But Ben did mind, and told her firmly that he wouldn't let her go until she'd had at least one cup of tea.

'I'll have it all ready in a few moments,' Mrs Bruton said. Stooping down to give Pippa a little hug, she asked, 'Will you come with me, pet?'

The child smiled back at her as if they were really the best of friends. The woman certainly didn't seem in the least like the dreaded Maggie Flute of her story.

When Pippa didn't move Mrs Bruton asked patiently, 'Well, are you coming or not?'

'I'll come,' Pippa said, dimpling at her, 'but only if I can hold Basil's lead.'

'Will that be all right, Dr Frinton?' the woman asked, then looked doubtfully at Ben.

'She can if you help her,' Ben said. 'The dog's much too strong for Pippa on her own.'

There was a stern warning in Ben's voice, which Kate thought quite unnecessary. Suddenly irritated, she said sharply, 'Basil's really very gentle.'

'With you maybe. But what happens if he suddenly runs off with Pippa?'

'He won't. He always does as he's told.' Kate frowned, staring at him and wondering why he seemed so intent on spoiling the child's pleasure. As Mrs Bruton left them and began to wander towards the house she said sharply, 'What gives you the right to dictate to Pippa like this?'

Ben looked at her with sudden fury, and as she saw tears in the child's eyes again Kate was angered by his injustice. 'What is it about you and dogs? Why do you dislike them so much?' she asked sharply.

'It's not a question of whether I like them or not,' he growled. 'I should have thought that you, as a doctor, would be fully aware of the health hazards. Don't you know that animals like this are banned from beaches, and even from some parks in this area?'

'Maybe. But there's no need to give this little love such a hard time! He's my dog, and I'll take him where I like.'

Tears were now running down Pippa's face again, and Kate suddenly blamed herself for them. 'I'm sorry, Ben,' she said. 'I shouldn't have lost my rag like that. I went too far. But I was only sticking up for Pippa.'

He gave her a little sideways smile. 'As impetuous as always, I see. How many times have I warned you about that?'

'Many! But you also said you wouldn't want me to change.'

'Fair enough. If you promise to guard your tongue a bit more then I might give in.' When Kate just stared silently at him again he urged, 'Go on, tell Pippa she can hold onto that animal with the ridiculous name.'

He called Mrs Bruton back. As Pippa took the lead

she looked up at Kate with eyes filled with love. 'I like you,' she said shyly. 'I'm going to put you in a story.'

'Thank you, sweetheart. That will be lovely,' Kate said softly.

Then she watched as Basil and Pippa walked sedately towards the house, with Mrs Bruton helping. The child and the dog looked so proud they could easily have been mistaken for a princess taking her royal greyhound for an airing, Kate thought. After all, hadn't Gordon Crisp once called him a prince of a dog?

At last Kate turned to Ben and asked, 'Whose little girl is she? A neighbour's child? I'd really like to meet her parents—to thank them for all the entertainment their daughter has given me.'

Ben looked at Kate in silence for a long time.

Then he leant towards her and said, 'You can thank me, Katie—because Pippa belongs to me. She's my daughter.'

CHAPTER TWELVE

BEWILDERED, Kate stared at Ben speechlessly. How could Pippa be his daughter? He'd told her about his wife drowning, but had never once mentioned a child.

Then she caught her breath as she remembered Ben speaking briefly of an elderly man and a child who had been swimming with them. At first she'd thought this man was the child's grandfather. She'd even wondered why he'd left the beach on his own.

It was Ben who'd rescued the child, wasn't it? Now Kate realised that the child must have been a girl because he said he'd rushed from the sea with 'her'.

'It was Pippa you saved the day your wife died, wasn't it?' she asked.

He nodded silently, and a great sadness filled her. For him and for all the suffering he had felt that day, and must still be feeling.

Then, strangely, bitterness began to move in her and she felt the cold ice of anger deep inside because he hadn't told her all this before. She knew it was unreasonable to feel pity and anger at the same time but she just couldn't help it.

'Yes. My daughter,' Ben said at last, his voice harsh. 'She was just a toddler then. Born with a damaged hip. It had been treated by surgery, of course. And had improved a little, but not enough. Then we found that exercising in water helped.' He paused, and she saw an unbridled agony moving deep in his eyes before he said, 'When that damned wind blew up from nowhere Janice and I were teaching her to swim.'

As she watched him Kate's anger suddenly died. And so did the unreasonable jealously she had felt when she'd imagined another woman living here besides the house-keeper. That beautiful, perfect creature had never existed, had she? The other person really waiting for Ben to return each night was Pippa!

Yet she couldn't rid herself of the pain that was still hurting deep inside her. She had thought Ben had trusted her enough to be honest with her. But he hadn't.

'Does Pippa remember her mother, even though she was just a toddler then?' she asked, her voice sounding as bleak as her thoughts.

'I think she must do because someone like Janice comes into the stories she invents.' He sighed, looking as if he didn't want to say any more. But eventually he forced himself to continue. 'It was since that time she began to speak nonsense. And developed temper tantrums. I hoped they would eventually leave her, but they never have.'

'She had one while I was with her,' Kate said quietly. 'But, Ben—they're not just tantrums. Pippa's anger is real—and has a very real cause.'

He stared at her, looking as if he were about to speak again, but Kate interrupted. 'I think she hides beneath that secret language, Ben. It expresses something that's important to her. Anger and fear—and loneliness, per-haps. Yet she thinks that if you really understood what she's saying you'd be disappointed in her.'

'What rubbish! Speaking nonsense is just a little game

she plays. All children go in for make-believe.'

'They do. But this isn't just a game, Ben,' Kate insisted. 'It's real to her. And very necessary.'

'You're telling me that her inner thoughts are hidden beneath all that—gobbledegook?'

'Yes, Ben. So why not encourage her to speak her thoughts in English? Then show her that however bad they may be you'll never be angry with her.'

He stayed silent, an obstinate look coming into his eyes. And the anger she had been repressing suddenly flared up in her again.

'Why in God's name didn't you tell me about her before?' she asked savagely. 'Did you find me so airheaded that I wouldn't understand? Might even accuse you of neglecting her because you leave her in the sole care of a middle-aged housekeeper?'

She saw him wince, then his own anger rose as he muttered, 'How can you say that, Kate? It's unjust. And it's cruel.'

'I can say it quite easily,' she said harshly. 'You've never been really straight with me, have you? You tell me so much, and no more. You ease your conscience by confessing how your wife died—but only speak when it pleases you. Why didn't you trust me enough to tell me about your daughter, Ben? It was unkind of you to keep silent. Hurtful.'

As he stared at her without answering her bitterness grew. No longer able to keep her voice from rising, she said tersely, 'Did you imagine I'd think any less of you for having a daughter who's been damaged? Do you keep her hidden here because you're ashamed of her, for God's sake?'

He went on staring at her, his face ravaged by the struggle that was going on deep inside him. But at last he said brokenly, 'I'm sorry, Kate—I should have told you.' Then his voice grew savage as he said, 'But I'm not ashamed of Pippa. Never have been. And it horrifies me that you could even think such a thing!'

She stretched a hand towards him then drew it back— suddenly afraid of him and his swiftly changing moods. As he turned away he told her brusquely to follow him to the house for the promised cup of tea, and she did as she was asked. But there was no joy in her.

Tea turned out to be not just a cup, but a real spread— with sandwiches, slices of cherry cake and scones with cream and jam. It was served in a breakfast room filled with knick-knacks Kate thought must belong to Pippa.

Colourful seashells were arranged artistically among exotic feathers that had once belonged to jays and pea-cocks. On a small shelf near a grandfather clock there was a collection of miniature ornaments—some made from coral, carved into little houses and animals, while others were plaster replicas of acrobats and dancers, all twirling around a tiny barrel organ.

'How lovely!' Kate exclaimed as she sat at a round table between Ben and Pippa. 'Were you the little girl who collected all these pretty things, sweetheart?'

Pippa nodded, looking pleased with herself. Then she suddenly giggled as Basil sniffed around and then pushed himself against her chair, sitting as close to her as he could possibly get.

'I wish Basil was mine,' she said in a wistful little voice as Mrs Bruton poured out from a silver teapot, then offered Kate a plate of sandwiches.

'Well, the dog isn't yours, thank goodness,' Ben said irritably. And Kate saw Pippa's eyes suddenly glimmer with tears.

Did he have to be so harsh with her? Kate couldn't risk saying what she really thought at that moment, but she did manage to give him a frown.

He saw it, and his face coloured as he said, 'You already know what I think of dogs mixing with humans. So there's no need to look at me like that, Kate, hiding what you really think. Why don't you come out with it?'

Wondering if it would be wise to say what she wanted to, Kate forced herself to look him straight in the eyes and said, 'I think a pet of some kind might help Pippa. She seems so lonely.'

'That's utter nonsense! She has Mrs Bruton for company, doesn't she? And, as I've said before, because you're a doctor you really should recognise the health hazard all animals present to humans.'

'So you don't subscribe to the theory that by stroking an animal's fur blood pressure can be dramatically lowered?'

'Oh, I know some doctors think that,' he said impatiently, 'but it doesn't stop the risk of infection, does it?'

Mrs Bruton suddenly interrupted. 'Could you talk about all this later?' she suggested, nodding towards Pippa whose tears were now threatening to spill down her cheeks.

Kate immediately stretched out both hands to the child, and felt her cling to them as if she were clutching at a lifeline. Now Ben's face was filled with guilt, and he opened his arms wide to his daughter.

But Pippa took no notice of him so Kate said, 'Why don't you ask your daddy to bring you to my flat one day? You can help me take Basil for a walk.' She turned to Ben and said coldly, 'Surely that wouldn't break your hard and fast rules, would it?'

He shrugged. 'If that's the way you want it then, yes, I'll bring Pippa to see you. When do you propose to begin this—therapy?'

'It's entirely up to you,' Kate said. Seeing Pippa's watery smile, she added, 'But don't leave it too long.'

When tea was finished Kate stood up, thanked Mrs Bruton for the delicious food and, taking Basil's lead, dropped a kiss on Pippa's forehead as she prepared to leave.

'I'll drive you to where you've left your car,' Ben said.

'Thank you, but there's really no need.'

'Yes, there is. This area is pretty deserted. Besides, you took the trouble to come all this way with Maurice's message, so the least I can do is to see you safely into your car.'

Even now he didn't smile at her. After dropping her where she had parked, he waited while she started the engine. Then he sped off, still wearing a frown.

The next afternoon Kate attended the interviews with a sinking heart, wondering what sort of cloud would be hanging over Ben. But she needn't have worried. The man sitting beside her was once more the professional colleague, whose obvious authority was tempered by good manners. When the candidates had been questioned closely and then told to wait in the corridor for a decision,

Kate was pleased to find herself completely in agreement with Ben's choice.

Afterwards, more mellow than she'd seen him for a long time, he took her aside and suggested they went out to tea together before her evening surgery. She refused.

'That's a pity,' he said. 'I thought we could talk some more.'

'Why? I thought you'd said it all.'

'I have. It's your turn now.'

'Oh, no, you're not going to get at me that way,' she said firmly.

'Why not? Fair's fair, isn't it? I reckon it's my turn to listen.'

'To what?'

'To the things that make you tick. And why you seem to hide your real feelings so often.'

Knowing that she couldn't trust herself to be alone him, she said, 'Sorry! I really am too busy to stop for tea just now.'

'How about after your surgery this evening, then? I could do with some of your special Dutch coffee.'

'No can do, I'm afraid,' she said. Then fled.

After that, Kate didn't see Ben for some time. Summer was now drawing to a close, with a hint of autumn already in the air. As darkness seemed to come earlier each night she realised that it wasn't just pressure of work which kept Ben away. He was deliberately ignoring her again. Now she regretted being so short with him after the interviews. Yet in a perverse kind of way she was pleased that he no longer seemed to have time for her. At least it gave her a chance to put him and his daughter into some sort of perspective.

Then something quite unexpected happened, taking away all her peace of mind.

One Wednesday evening, returning home early from the Well Woman Clinic where there had seemed to be fewer patients than usual, Kate decided to put her feet up and do absolutely nothing after supper. But just as she was washing up her front doorbell rang—and went on ringing until she ran down the stairs.

It was now almost dark so she put the chain on the door, before opening it cautiously. She caught her breath as she saw Ben standing there. He was peering through the crack and looking so anxious that she immediately opened the door wide to him.

'What's happened?' she asked breathlessly, catching his uneasiness. 'I thought you were sitting at The Rowans tonight.'

'I was, but Maurice is standing in for me. Something terrible has happened.'

'An accident? Do you want me to come with you?'

'No, nothing like that. I just came to ask if Pippa's here with you.'

'*What*? No, of course not. Why should she be?'

'Because just before she went to bed she apparently asked Mrs Bruton where you lived. When the house-keeper checked on her later, as she always does every night, the child had vanished. Just like that!'

'Oh, Ben, how awful!

'It is,' he said brusquely. 'Mrs Bruton rang me at The Rowans the moment she found the bed empty, and

Maurice sent me off to look for her. The first place I could think of was your flat.'

'But Pippa just couldn't come all this way on her own. And why would she want to?'

'Because of your damned dog,' he snapped. 'She's always on about him, asking when you'll be taking her for a walk with him. Even telling Mrs Bruton she's seen him in the garden. Do you think he could have got out and found his way to my house?'

'Of course not. That's ridiculous!'

'Then why should Pippa say she's seen him?'

'She must have imagined it.'

'And the animal has never run away?' Ben asked sharply.

'Never!'

'How can you be so sure?'

'Because when he isn't with me in the car he's asleep in his basket in the sitting room.'

'How about now? Can you swear he's still here?'

'Of course I can!' Kate felt herself growing impatient. 'Come up and see for yourself, if you doubt me.'

Ben glanced up the stairs, then smiled ruefully as he said, 'There's no need. Look!'

Basil had suddenly appeared and was now doing his usual dignified walk as he descended to the hall. Then he sat down, giving his one-bark greeting before looking at them curiously as if he thought them both mad.

'I'm sorry I doubted you,' Ben said, giving her a wan sort of half-smile.

'That's OK. But Basil being here doesn't really solve your problem, does it? Can you think of anything else Pippa said to Mrs Bruton?'

'No. Just that she wanted to see the dog and knew where to find him. Can you think of anything else, Kate?'

'No. Unless. . .' Kate saw hope rising in him, and hesitated. If she told him what she was thinking it might easily lead to disappointment.

'Go on,' he said urgently. 'What were you going to say?'

She sighed. 'It may be nothing, Ben. But when I first met Pippa she asked me to tell her a story about Basil. So I described the way we'd come through the copse, and how he sat by a rabbit hole, waiting patiently for something to appear.'

Ben stared at her in silence for a moment. Then he said urgently, 'Come on! We'll go there at once. Let's take Basil with us, and re-enact the scene if we have to. I've got a powerful torch in the car so don't worry, we won't get lost.'

To Kate this seemed the height of insanity, but she did as he asked. Clipping the lead to Basil's collar, she took him to Ben's car where she sat in the front seat with the dog resting against her legs. Then Ben was driving to the place she would always think of as his 'magic wood'.

There was bright moonlight, even shining through the densest part of the copse, so Kate was able to lead the way without the use of Ben's torch. When they reached the very rabbit hole Basil had found that day he again sat down in front of it, once more refusing to be budged.

Ben peered at the animal in amazement, then asked, 'Is this it?'

'Yes, I'm sure. But I don't really know how this is going to help.'

Ben suddenly held up a hand, then whispered, 'Listen! Can you hear anything?'

'Just a breeze stirring the trees. And a kind of rustling, like birds being disturbed,' Kate said.

Then she heard something else. A crackle of twigs that seemed to get louder as someone walked steadily towards them. She clutched Ben's arm as a shiver of fear suddenly touched her skin. Basil began barking with excitement.

Ben snapped on his torch, playing its light along the ground. Kate saw a glimmer of something white coming towards them.

'For God's sake, what is it?' she whispered hoarsely.

Ben chuckled quietly. 'I think it's someone wearing a nightdress,' he said.

A moment later Kate heard Pippa's voice calling, 'Daddy! Daddy!' Then she watched the child hurl her small body into Ben's open arms.

'There, there, my little love,' he said as he stroked the tangle of dark curls. 'Can you tell us what you're doing here?'

In the moonlight Kate saw surprise in the child's eyes. 'I'm looking for Basil, of course. Now I've found him!' She was struggling in her father's arms, trying to get near Basil who was making pitiful whining noises as he pulled against his lead. 'I knew I would if I looked hard enough!'

Ben let her go, and she gave Kate a shy kiss. 'Thank you for bringing him,' she said. Then she was kneeling with her arms clasped round the dog as they both peered into the rabbit hole. 'Is this the place, Basil?' she asked, and looked as if she'd gone straight to heaven when Basil licked her gently on the cheek.

Horrified by what Ben might say about this, Kate pulled on the lead and told Basil to behave himself.

But Ben just laughed softly. 'Don't worry, my Katie!' he said huskily. 'I'd rather see Pippa happy than find her in tears. Or not even find her at all.'

'But—what about all those germs?' Kate asked, amazed by this turn-around.

'Pippa can always wash her face, can't she?' He grinned at her as he carried his daughter in his arms towards the clearing.

When he saw Kate lagging behind with Basil, he waited for her to catch up. 'Why are you hanging back like that?' he asked.

'I—well, I didn't want to intrude. The two of you seem so. . .complete.'

'That's nonsense, my Katie,' he said softly, setting Pippa on her feet again. Then, after telling her to go to the house to let Mrs Bruton know she was safe, he said, 'We'll never be really whole without you.'

'What do you mean, Ben?'

'Can't you guess?'

She stared at him in the moonlight, watching a myriad expressions dancing in his eyes. Then she said quietly, 'Are you saying that you actually—love me?'

'Yes, my Katie. I fought against it for a long, long time. You see, I thought I just couldn't expect any woman to put up with me, and all the darkness and guilt that's been inside me since Janice went.'

He paused for a moment, his eyes becoming shadowed again. Then he said, 'Besides, I knew I couldn't share

Pippa with someone who would never understand what that child has been through. That is, until I saw how much she likes you. And how patient you are with her. Now I've lost the battle, and I don't want to fight any more.'

'But I thought. . .'

'That it was just something physical between us?' She nodded miserably. He said softly, 'Come here, my love. Let me wrap my arms around you and tell you how I felt from the moment I saw you. How I tried to ignore the love that almost made my heart stop the first time your green eyes looked into mine.'

She dropped Basil's lead, and he went trotting after Pippa. As Ben's arms crept around her she looked up at him in the moonlight. 'There's a lot you don't know about me, Ben. Unhappy things I've never told you, even though I knew I was being unfair to you, expecting you to be open with me.'

'Do you think I don't realise that, my Katie? I've seen the struggle inside you, and have wanted you to tell me about it many times. But if you wish to keep it from me I'll respect that privacy you've always guarded so fiercely.'

'No, Ben. I don't want any more secrets between us. I must tell you.'

Then she deliberately summoned up all those painful memories of David, and at last spoke of him aloud. Something she had never done before.

Feeling the comfort of Ben's arms around her, she told him how David had always wanted to dominate her. How she had given in for the sake of peace. And how she'd finally realised that he was obsessed with power—not with love.

'So how did it end, my Katie?' he asked softly.

She took in a shuddering breath and said, 'He found I wasn't willing to—become his slave. That sounds ridiculous, doesn't it? But that's the way he wanted me to be. When I fought against it he—he beat me up. Yes, actually attacked me. Abused me. Pitting his strength against my weakness.'

'My little love,' Ben murmured, brushing soft lips against her cheek. 'Let me comfort you. Make you forget all that agony—as you have made me forget mine.'

'It's so strange, Ben. What happened to me in the past suddenly doesn't seem important any more. You've begun to heal me, Ben. Just like the good doctor you are!' Kate sighed, then said, 'I'd like to stop talking about all this now. If I don't, the magic of this wonderful place will be spoilt.'

She could see his eyes glinting silver in the moonlight. As his arms tightened around her and his lips met hers, she felt herself melting beneath his kiss.

At last he lifted his lips from hers, and his voice was urgent as he said, 'Marry me, Kate! Please marry me, my darling. If you don't I think I might well end up as a crabby old man!'

'I won't let you,' she said, smiling up at him.

'Does that mean—yes?'

'It does,' she said, her voice no louder than a whisper.

Suddenly they heard Mrs Bruton's voice saying, 'So, you found Pippa at last! I never thought of looking in the wood. But thank goodness you did!'

As Ben released Kate the housekeeper walked towards

them, somehow managing to hold Pippa's hand and
Basil's lead at the same time. There was a smile on her
face, made quite angelic by the moonlight. Handing the
dog to Kate, she said, 'It's nice to see you again, Dr
Frinton. Would you like to come in for a hot drink before
you go home?'

'Lovely!' Kate said, still feeling in a glorious daze.

Then Ben said, 'It won't be long before Dr Frinton
lives here permanently. You see, we're going to be
married.'

'Well done, Dr Ben!' Mrs Bruton chuckled. 'But I
must say it has come as no surprise to me.'

As the housekeeper went towards the house to make
the hot drinks Pippa stared at them both, and Kate began
to feel nervous.

But she needn't have worried. For, after giving them
a smile that seemed quite huge in the moonlight, the
child clung to Kate and hugged her.

'Will Basil live here too?' she asked.

'Of course, my little love,' Ben said.

'What? No qualms about germs?' Kate asked with
a grin.

'What do you think?'

With that, Ben caught hold of Basil's lead and, stretching one arm round Kate, he helped Pippa to walk the
dog towards the house.

Then, sitting graciously by one of the long windows,
Basil lifted his head and gave his famous one-bark
comment.

Just as if he already lived here, Kate thought with
a smile.

We hoped you have enjoyed this month's Medical Romances™ from our 'Rising Stars'—four talented new authors.

To ensure we continue to provide you with the very best in Medical Romances, please spare a few minutes to answer the following questions. Your comments are very much appreciated. Please tick the appropriate box to indicate your answers.

THINKING ABOUT THE MEDICAL ROMANCE STORYLINES, IS THERE:

1. Too much medical content ❑
   Not enough ❑
   Just right ❑

2. Are the medical references too technical? ❑
   Not technical enough ❑
   Just right ❑

3. Are the stories: Too sensual ❑
   Not sensual enough ❑
   Just right ❑

4. Do you like settings in the UK ❑
   Foreign Countries ❑
   Don't mind ❑

5. Do you like stories that are linked to other books?
   e.g. Flying Doctors, Camberton Hospital   Y ❑   N ❑

6. How long have you been a Medical Romance reader?
   Less than 1 year ❑   1-2 years ❑   3-5 years ❑
   6-10 years ❑   Over 10 years ❑

7. Do you read any other Mills & Boon® series?
   Please tick the series you read   Presents™ ❑
   Enchanted™ ❑
   Historical Romance™ ❑
   Temptation® ❑
   By Request™ ❑
   Others (please specify) ❑

8. How many Medical Romances™ do you read/buy in a month?

Read	Buy
1-4 ❑	❑
5-8 ❑	❑
9-12 ❑	❑
13-16 ❑	❑

9. Thinking about the new white Medical Romance covers, do you:
Like it very much ❑   Don't like it very much ❑
Like it quite a lot ❑   Don't like it at all ❑

10. Please indicate your age group
16-24 ❑   25-34 ❑   35-44 ❑
45-54 ❑   55-64 ❑   65+ ❑

THANK YOU FOR YOUR HELP

Please send your completed questionnaire to:

Harlequin Mills & Boon
Medical Romance Questionnaire
Dept M
PO Box 183, Richmond
Surrey, TW9 1ST

Ms/Mrs/Miss/Mr _____

Address: _____

_____

_____ Postcode _____

You may be mailed with offers form other reputable
companies as a result of this application.
If you would prefer not to receive such offers,
please tick box. ❑

MILLS & BOON®

Medical Romance™

COMING NEXT MONTH

INCURABLY ISABELLE by Lilian Darcy

Isabelle returns to her roots in France, determined to heal a long-standing family rift, but, made apprehensive by a friend, she keeps her identity secret from her second cousin, Jacques—a mistake, when they fell in love.

HEART OF GOLD by Jessica Matthews
Sisters at Heart

Kirsten is committed to her clinic helping the poor, but its future is uncertain. She reluctantly accepts the help of Jake, unaware he is responsible for the uncertainty.

FIRST THINGS FIRST by Josie Metcalfe
St Augustine's

Nick can't face the anniversary of his wife's death; Polly won't let him give in, but when did comforting turn into love?

WINGS OF LOVE by Meredith Webber
Flying Doctors—final episode

Base Manager Leonie had survived one bad marriage—loving Alex was a risk, one she might not take, particularly if it meant living in Italy!

Meet
A PERFECT FAMILY

Shocking revelations and heartache lie just beneath the surface of their charmed lives.

The Crightons are a family in conflict. Long-held resentments and jealousies are reawakened when three generations gather for a special celebration.

One revelation leads to another - a secret war-time liaison, a carefully concealed embezzlement scam, the illicit seduction of another's wife. The façade begins to crack, revealing a family far from perfect, underneath.

"Women everywhere will find pieces of themselves in Jordan's characters"

–Publishers Weekly

The coupon is valid only in the UK and Eire against purchases made in retail outlets and not in conjunction with any Reader Service or other offer.